WILD HORSE GORGE

WILD HORSE GORGE

•

Duncan Ross

AVALON BOOKS
NEW YORK

Library of Congress Catalog Card Number: 00-100786
ISBN 0-8034-9431-9

Published by Thomas Bouregy & Co., Inc.
160 Madison Avenue, New York, NY 10016

PRINTED IN THE UNITED STATES OF AMERICA
ON ACID-FREE PAPER
BY HADDON CRAFTSMEN, BLOOMSBURG, PENNSYLVANIA

For Lauren, Michael, and Sarah

Chapter One

"I think that wild horses have more secrets than gentle ones."

—J. Frank Dobie, *The Mustangs*

Washington Marion Buchanan kicked the foam-lathered stallion up a steep bank and reined to a stop. Like his mount, the man was sweat-stained, his heart pounding. He had ridden the thoroughbred hard all morning, he knew the horse was tired. But it was time to test him. See if he really had the speed and stamina they hoped.

Gathering the reins tightly in his left hand, Wash Buchanan leaned forward, booted his heels to the horse's flanks and yelled, "Okay, Boy. Let's go!"

As soon as boots hit flank, the stallion lunged down the embankment. Stretching his long neck toward the trees half a mile away, he gathered speed with every leap. Pistoned by iron-shanked shoulders, he clawed at the approaching earth. His hind-quarters followed with a heave that sent rider and horse flying over the sun-baked field.

Wash grabbed for his hat, missing it, he grinned as it blew away.

Never had he ridden so fast. And he had ridden many horses. Since he was a ten-year-old orphaned by the great war, he had lived and worked with his uncle in the Buchanan stables. Together they had built a reputation for training and breeding the best saddle and buggy horses in St. Louis.

They had raised promising colts and sold them for above-market prices. And they had kept a few for their own needs. But until Jones McFadden sold them the ailing red stallion for a paltry sum—expecting him to die within the night—they had never had such a horse.

The huge stallion stood sixteen hands high with the large alert eye that denoted inherent intelligence. He had a lineage that reached back six generations and a name to go with it, Hoshaba The One. Wash had raised eyebrows when Jones McFadden told him the name. "Hoshaba was the Arabian stud who founded the thoroughbred line, you see," McFadden said. "Way back, too many years ago to count." The man had wagged his head at his loss.

Now, racing ever nearer those trees, Wash could hardly breathe. The hot afternoon air whistling down his throat threatened to cut off his wind. He pulled on the reins.

Hoshaba paid no attention. Instead, he clamped the softly curved bit between his teeth and sped toward to the trees. *Hell's Fire!* Wash thought, *we'll be beheaded under those low limbs!*

Again he yanked on the reins, this time "Whoaing!" with anxiety about to become a yell.

That long neck continued to reach, the legs to glide over the earth. Wash's heart beat faster. He reached for an ear. A painful pinch and tug on a sensitive ear had stopped runaways before. Maybe it would work this time.

Then a rabbit popped up directly in their path and the great red stallion swerved aside, skidding with outstretched legs, and ground to a halt ten feet shy of the elms.

Wash Buchanan closed sand-burned eyes and slumped in the saddle. He sighed with relief. Then he began to laugh. "What a ride, you old son-of-a-gun!" he cried. "You'll do. Yea, you'll do!"

Jake Buchanan coughed until blood spotted his handkerchief. Nodding at the reality of it, he cleared his throat, then poked at the coals glowing red in the ancient iron cook stove. "Git them biscuits under your belt, Wash. I got somethin' to show you."

Wash poured syrup over the hot biscuits and began to eat, downing each bite with gulps of thick black coffee. "I have something to tell *you*, Jake. About that horse."

"He run good today?" the old man asked, struggling to stifle another cough.

"Did he! He's fit and faster than we ever dreamed. Doctoring with that stinking black concoction of yours brought him back strong as a mule. If Jones McFadden could see him now he'd kick himself through a thousand Sundays."

Jake slapped a palm on the table top. "Hee yeow! I told you he were a good'un. Now all you gotta do is pack your bags."

"Jake." Wash began.

"No, now jest hold your taters, son. This here telegram

will change your mind." He fumbled a paper from his shirt pocket and handed it across the table. "Rode into town whilst you wus out and sure 'nuff, I'd got me an answer from your granpa."

Wash pushed back his chair and sat forward, rubbing stiff fingers through his short black hair. He wanted nothing to do with his mother's father. The man had disowned her when she needed him. When she begged him to bless her and her man before they left for Philadelphia, he wouldn't. Instead he sent her off saying he never wanted to see her again.

It was too late now for making up.

Jake shook his finger at the telegram. "Read it, Washington. The tele man read it to me but I want to hear it agin'."

Wash knew the old man would not give up. Anger rising in his belly, he yanked up the message and began to read. "Glad to hear I have a grandson stop tell him all is forgiven stop I have 2000 acres stop am changing my will today stop He gets it all stop. Signed, Francis Marion Ross, Granite Canyon, Wyoming."

Before Wash could react his uncle sputtered, "Don't that beat all? Here we wus hoping maybe he'd allow us to visit whilst we found a place to start up our ranch . . . and . . . and he laid a gold mine right plum in our laps."

"*Your* ranch, uncle Jake. It's your idea, your dream. Not mine," Wash said, exasperated at his stubbornness. "Besides, I keep reminding you it's nothing new. Baxter Sinclair, over near Ponder, just had a foal from a good saddle horse he'd bred to a little Indian mustang mare he bought. Your idea isn't new, Jake."

With his head lowered, Wash glanced up at his uncle. "And as for asking Granpa Ross for help . . . you know

I want nothing to do with a man who would disown a daughter simply because she wanted to marry and move away."

Jake Buchanan was not perturbed. His rheumy eyes lit up as usual when he spoke of it. "That there foal Sinclair had. It will be better than its ma and pa put together. You wait. And Washington, we're going to do it different. We're doing it agin' and agin' til we have a whole new kind o' stock, a mix you can count on to reproduce in kind."

Jake stopped to stand in the doorway and cough. When his chest quit heaving he turned and said with hurry blurring his words, "And you know yourself, lad, there's not another stud like this'n comin' along in a dog's age."

Wash was shaking his head but it had no effect on Jake Buchanan. The old man sat down at the table and leaned close. "Now that Red is fit, we can leave. Lars wants the stable, he's rarin' to take over. That there jar under the cabinet is full o' gold twenties . . . enough to keep us for a year. And Washington," his hand shook as he lifted it in the air, "If we don't do it soon. . . ."

Wash Buchanan blew out his breath. He stood up and went over to the tall pie safe that had long ago become a haven for his books. He picked up THE TALISMAN by Walter Scott. It was worn on the edges, its pages smudged by a thousand dirty fingers. Wash's father had given it to him for his eighth birthday. They had read it and re-read it together over the next three years until John Buchanan had gone to war and died at Antietam. " 'Bring honour away or remain with the dead. . . .' " Wash whispered.

Jake grumped. "You and your quotes. You still miss

your pa, don't you. I do some too. He wus a right good brother though we growed up differnt. He studying and being a teacher, me staying on the place and learnin' horse ways.

"But, Wash, you have some o' your grandad Ross in you too. Whether you want it or not. He did only whut he knowed best when he told your ma not to marry John Buchanan. Now he's come to admit his wrong, don't let him die without seein' you."

Beside the books leaned the tintype of a young woman sitting beside a handsome soldier holding a rifle. Wash's glance centered on that tall, evil gun. He loathed it. His mother had told him time and again how one like it had snuffed out the life of her beloved husband, his father.

Wash touched the face of his mother in the picture. She was dark-eyed, with skin that smelled of rosebuds. He remembered how she always patted his hand as if everything was all right when she spoke about her father.

When he turned to face Jake he wore a defeated smile. "And don't let the opportunity of breeding a thoroughbred stallion to a passel of wild mustangs go by the way?"

Jake's eyes lit up. He grinned. "Yea, that too."

Three weeks later Wash stood beside the grave of his uncle Jake. A fever had hit the lung-scarred man and within ten days he was dead. Why now? Wash wondered as a hard knot swelled inside his chest. Why after all these years of dreaming he would someday "go out west" and breed wild mustangs with a good eastern horse, did it have to end now.

Wash stooped to place a rusty, bent horseshoe atop the pile of earth. "Sweet dreams, ol'-timer," he whispered. "And remember, your dream will be coming true down here at the same time. I'm taking Hoshaba to Wyoming in a special railcar just like you wanted. We'll make a deal with granpa Ross for land . . . and we'll round up a bunch of mustang mares. Before you know it we'll have us the finest bunch of Buchanan and Buchanan saddle ponies anyone ever saw.

"Hoshaba and I are leaving next week, Jake. So you look down from up there and watch for us. You hear? Watch for us."

Wash backed away from the lump of ground that held the man who had been his only family for the last twelve years.

Yes, he thought, *I'll go out to that old man, Francis Marion Ross. But I won't like it.*

A grandfather who lived half a continent and more than a lifetime away . . . was no one to him.

Chapter Two

At Cheyenne Wyoming the train made its last stop before Granite Canyon. Wash got off to stretch his legs and check on Hoshaba. Hopping off his coach, he hurried toward the cattle cars at the rear of the train.

"Hey! Hold up there! This is a private car. Get those cattle back!" he yelled, horrified at the sight. He shouldered a path through a tangle of bawling cattle being driven up a loading platform into the stock car. He waved at one of the cowhands to stop as the man reined his horse to drive half a dozen laggers into the herd.

"Stop!" Wash was frantic . . . and blood-boiling angry. Didn't they realize what they were doing? "Close that door. Turn those cows back. No more. No more!"

Two cowhands on foot at the rear of the herd swirled ropes and whistled. Bunching the cows together they pushed them toward the ramp. In disbelief, Wash grabbed the shirt front of the nearest man and jerking him around yelled in his ear, "Can't you understand? No cattle in this car!"

"Out o' the way, Mister!" the cowboy snarled, and pushed Wash aside.

Wash saw red. Those cattle would kill his horse . . . or maim him. He leapt onto the cowboy's back and together they tumbled into the dirt under hooves and horns. Hitting, scrabbling for a foothold, they scrambled to one side where Wash drove his head into the gut of the man who bent double, coughing and gagging.

Another man joined and Wash whirled to lay a fist into the man's nose. Blood spurted and he leaned against the corral rail, cursing and dripping blood.

Then a huge brute of a creature with a bald head, grabbed Wash around the waist. With an iron-lock on his chest, he pulled him away. As he did, his ham-fists closed around the moneybelt Wash wore. Wrestling Wash to a standstill, he grinned down at a man coming toward them.

"What's the trouble here?" The man was dressed in a red silk shirt and busily smoking a cigar.

"Mr. Whelper, he just started fighting," Bloody-nose offered. "For some reason he didn't want those cattle loaded."

Wash yanked free from the hold of the brute who nodded at Whelper and eased back. Wash was hot, and dirty, and breathing hard. "Are you the man that ordered these cattle into this car?" he demanded.

Whelper sucked on the cigar. "Yes, I am. The car was empty. Except for one horse, which I suppose by your lather is yours."

"Weren't you informed this car was reserved . . . private, not to be used?" Wash asked curtly, turning to see the last of the cattle shoved in.

Jack Whelper tossed his cigar, his jaw tightening. "No car is private in this country whenever there's cattle need moving. And mine need moving! Besides, your horse is all right. We put up a good pine pole fence to hold him."

Suddenly a piercing scream broke from the car as the door closed. The cry from Hoshaba churned Wash's gut into a knot. Without thinking he surged toward Whelper. With a doubled up fist he swung a round-house blow into Whelper's chest. The man stumbled, fell backward into the chalky dust, and before any of the men could move, had pulled a .45 from his coat. Leveling it at Wash he stammered through gritted teeth, "What the heck is wrong with you? Are you crazy?"

"Those cattle will kill my horse," Wash stated. "Get them out of there."

"You are crazy! I told you those cattle can't get to that horse!" Whelper clamped his teeth around his cigar and raised the gun.

Wash Buchanan stood looking down at the revolver in Whelper's shaking hand. He had never had a gun pulled on him. He had never owned a gun. He thought of the rifle in the picture of his father and wondered why men needed to shoot other men.

"Boss, wait," one of the cowhands sputtered, hesitating, evidently afraid to cross Whelper but not wanting a gun fight.

Then another man, a smaller version of Whelper and until now staying out of the fray, bent toward Whelper. Leaning close he whispered, "Not now, Jack. Let him be. We got the cattle in."

Jack Whelper lowered the .45. His eye still on Wash,

he allowed himself to be pulled up. He accepted his hat out of the dust from a third man, a tall, skinny, stoop-shouldered cuss who promptly put himself in front of the cattle ramp where he stood on guard.

Glaring at Wash with eyes squinting cold fury, Whelper slowly holstered his gun. He looked around at his men. "It's okay. The young man was just worried about his horse. Get back to work." Whelper said nothing to Wash but turned and walked off.

Wash wiped his mouth with the back of his hand and warned, "If that horse is hurt. . . ." He pushed Stoop-shoulder aside and bounded up the ramp. Opening the door he stood for a second letting his eyes adjust to the dim light. He stood tiptoe, studying the end of the car. When he saw the horse, relief flooded over him. The man had indeed built a fence. He'd used stout pine poles eight inches apart. They were tightly affixed to the sides of the railcar. The man should have come to him first. Maybe the fight would have been avoided.

Wash could not get through the clot of cattle, but he could tell the thoroughbred was okay. Hoshaba was standing wide-eyed, ears up, but he was not panicking. Like Whelper said, he was all right.

"It'll have to do, boy," Wash muttered and leaped off as the car began to rumble and jerk.

Once settled on the wooden bench in his coach car, Wash took a long, deep breath, forcing himself to relax. The sight of that .45 pointed at him had shaken him. He set his eye on the country passing by the window. The land was just as Jake said, free and open, and enough of it for all the horses any man would want.

He had been mesmerized by the wildflower-covered prairies and the blue hills in the distance. For the last few days he had soaked up the wonder of it, all the way to Cheyenne where Whelper had loaded his beeves. *Blast the man*, Wash thought. *He should have asked me. That fight was Whelper's fault.*

"Mr. Buchanan, we heard about your trouble with Jack Whelper." The young woman sitting opposite him was Elizabeth Drennan. She spoke with a directness he liked. But she was no western girl, she was a product of the East just as he was and quite as fashionable as any of the ladies in St. Louis. She wore her blond hair in the latest style, rolled up to circle her head and crowned with a hat of emerald green to match her eyes.

Her father snored beside her, his head thrown back and his mouth agape like a fat, sunning frog.

She continued, "Is that beautiful horse of yours safe?"

"I hope so," Wash said. "He'd better be. Do you know this Whelper guy?"

"Everyone in Granite Canyon knows Jack Whelper and his brother Lewis. They run a very large cattle operation. Those beeves he loaded at Cheyenne are going on to Fort Sanders. You know the army pays a premium for beef."

Her father grunted in his sleep and she leaned close to Wash as she added, "I should tell you, Mr. Buchanan, you made a very risky decision when you jumped Jack Whelper. He doesn't like to lose face."

"He didn't. He got his cattle in my car, didn't he?"

She smiled. "Yes, but he'll remember the stand-off. You must realize out here a man is held in esteem only if he can beat the other man. Whether it's by gun or fist or just playing the odds in a smarter way.

"I'm afraid you took some of that away from Mr. Whelper today."

"I'll leave him be from now on. I just want to start my own spread . . . and that will be with horses."

Elizabeth wiped her cheeks with a lace handkerchief as a gust of cinders blew in. "Oh," she realized suddenly. "Then that is where that beauty of a horse comes in, isn't it?"

"Yes it is. I intend to breed him to mustang mares."

"Really?"

"My uncle and I think . . . that is, he believed . . . the result would produce a better riding-working horse. Offspring usually have the stamina and hardiness of the mustang, along with the speed and size of the thoroughbred. I hope to start a line that will breed true to these qualities."

J. T. Drennan blinked awake. "Then you'll need wire, son." He sat up, not wanting to miss a sale. "I'm a representative for Haish's Barbed fencing wire." He reached into his case and pulled out a short strand of stiff wire. He thrust it toward Wash saying, "See this? It's a double, just like the Glidden . . . BUT, you'll notice this has an S curved sticker that weaves itself around both strands, thus becoming stationary."

When Wash merely stared, Drennan added, "That means an animal gets stuck . . . the sticker cuts into its hide . . . a steer or horse will not be going through the blasted fence."

J. T. Drennan carefully encased his trophy and said, "It's the latest thing, Mr. Buchanan, you'll want to use it when you get your place.

"You have your land yet?" he asked.

For a moment Wash couldn't find words. He'd never spoken of his grandfather to anyone besides Jake. It was as if he did not exist. "Maybe," he said. "I . . . that is, my grandfather, has a ranch north of Granite."

"That's wonderful country," Elizabeth said. "It has timber and water and those buttes to the west are marvelous." Then her green eyes darkened. "But, Mr. Buchanan, the east side of that land borders Jack Whelper's spread. He claims from the North Platte all the way to Cheyenne.

Wash felt a shiver of apprehension. Was he destined to confront the man? "I see," was all he could manage.

J. T. Drennan took out his watch. "We'll be in Granite any minute now. Say, Buchanan, meet us for supper some night at Delmonicos. We'll talk ranching and wiring." He pulled at the vest riding high on his bulging stomach and asked, "What's your grandfather's name? I didn't catch it."

"He's Francis Marion Ross. You know of him?"

A tiny gasp escaped Elizabeth's red-lipped mouth. She looked at her father then stared out the window. Wash waited for her to say something.

When she looked back, there were tears in her eyes. "Oh, Mr. Buchanan, we have heard of him. He . . . that is . . ."

Wash stiffened. Waited.

J. T. cleared his throat and said, "Sorry, son, but that old man died the day before we left for Omaha."

Chapter Three

"Be a spell 'fore your horse is out, Mr. Buchanan," declared a sooty-faced yardman who jumped onto the cattle car as it lurched backward. "He'll be unloaded at the corrals back that-aways."

"Thanks," Wash said and planting his hat on his head to keep off the boiling afternoon sun, he headed in that direction.

Wash felt confused and a little light-headed. The news of his grandfather's death was a shock. How could his two remaining kin die within weeks of each other? What would he do now? Where exactly was the ranch and how would he get there?

He swiped a hand across his face, wiping away the thoughts. He had too much to do before worrying about that.

He sauntered toward the back edge of the main shed and leaned against a pole in a small spot of shade. He wanted to watch the unloading. He knew about horses, but he knew nothing about cattle. He decided he'd better learn. His grandfather had cattle, didn't he?

From where he was he could see Whelper and his men standing just inside the shed to one side. Not moving, his hands clenched and hardened, readying without his bidding to do battle again. Wash shook his head. Would this be a place of continual struggle? Was it one of the reasons his mother wanted to leave this "violent country" as she always referred to it?

Whelper and his men spoke in low, guttural whispers. Wash could hear every word they said. ". . . The W will cover that big C real good, Jack. No hassle. It'll look just like a crooked-wise W." This came from the small man who was a miniature version of Jack. No doubt his brother, Lewis.

"Yea, boss, and we'll have another hunerd ready in a week," added a sun-burned cowpoke.

Suddenly the bald-headed brute glanced in Wash's direction, frowned for an instant then touched Jack Whelper on the arm. Whelper had changed to a green shirt and a new grey hat. He turned around and stared at Wash along with the brute.

Wash thought the man was going to confront him, but he turned and motioned his men away.

Near the first corral gate the train bucked to a stop. The door was pulled open and Jack Whelper's cattle stomped their way down the ramp and into the corral. Cowboys hooted and whistled and swung their ropes, herding the bawling critters along. A white, chalky dust swirled in chocking clouds around the whole yard. It clung to Wash's black boots and pants like whitewash.

The lean, work-hardened cowboys sat their ponies with ease. They kept their hands free for lariats, using only knees and boot heels to move their mounts, to work the cattle. They turned the cows, roped those that were ramming their horns, pushed a limping bull aside, and within minutes had the cattle circling, calming, settling for the night.

Good work, Wash thought. *Some day you'll be using horses bred at the Buchanan stables.*

Anxious now to see Hoshaba, he hurried into the dark, hot railcar.

An equally anxious horse greeted him with a whinny. His horse was safe behind the poles. At least Whelper's men appreciated good horseflesh. Wash pulled Hoshaba's halter around to see his face. Relief flooded over him when he saw its clear-eyed beauty. He slid his hands over the quivering shoulders and down the flinching belly. The legs too he checked.

"You're okay, boy," he said. "But let's get you out of here."

Wash left his two small trunks at the station. He'd pick them up later. He wanted to find a place to stable Hoshaba.

Halter in hand, he ambled down the one main street in Granite Canyon. Compared to St. Louis it was deserted. He noticed a few women bustling from store to bank, and a string of tobacco-spitting men sitting in the shade of the boardwalk awnings. But no one was in a hurry.

The saloon he passed looked cool and inviting inside, but he'd never been enticed by hard liquor. It left all the men he'd ever seen loose-tongued and careless. But there on his left was the Trail End Hotel. He'd need that at least for tonight.

From between two buildings a hassle of small boys

ran out, stopped, and ooing and ohhing, began to follow behind the thoroughbred. One danced up to Wash and asked, "Where'd you git that horse, Mister? He sure is big."

Wash nodded and kept going.

"He fast?"

"Fast enough," Wash answered with great seriousness.

"He ain't got no brand. You steal him?"

A shiver slid down Wash's neck. "No, I didn't steal him. I have papers on him."

"Better not let Mr. Whelper see him," the boy said with gusto and skipping in the dust, whipped out a hand to touch Hoshaba's flank. Hoshaba flipped his rear aside and blew through his nose.

Squealing with fear and delight, the boys fled into the alley.

A bright yellow sign over a heavy iron-barred door read: Shearif's Ooffice. Probably be going there too, Wash thought. I just hope he's a little more astute than his sign indicates. I'll need to find out from him about granpa Ross and what I should do.

Finally, when he had passed a mercantile and a saddlery and acknowledged several bug-eyed stares from two gentlemen types, he came to the end of the street. And to the open doors of Ed Lowery's Livery.

Chapter Four

The high country northwest of Granite Canyon, leading into the Black Hills, was a mass of rough-timbered buttes, rocky valleys, and brush-covered plateaus. A wild land of hellcat and snake. No decent civilized man had found pleasure putting it to seed or running stock on it. No settlers built corrals or houses or towns. It was a lonely place.

But being alone was what the man called Briley hankered for. Loneliness was soothing. A quieting thing for a man chased by hurt and regret and the fear of a posse closing in.

He had been over fifteen years trailing after a peace that he could never really get hold of. A peace he could not find to fill the empty hole in his gut where all his hopes and dreams lay.

Briley spent his waking hours alone with his thoughts, shutting out any intruding idea of a life with people. It was too risky living close to folk.

He went in to the sprawling town of Cheyenne every year to take his ore and to bank his money. That took several days of hard travel, there and back. But he was careful, he kept a watch on his backside and spoke only to the banker and the assayer.

In years past he had made many a trek hunting for a sign of Mary Rose and the child. But he knew now that was useless. Why, even then, soon after it happened, the man in Dry Springs had told him straight off he'd seen them, both sick and near dying, not able to last another day.

Somehow Briley had not wanted to believe they were dead and he had gone on searching.

But that was fifteen years ago.

Now Briley worked. He worked the mine from sun-up till the lantern gave out at night. He worked as if he had a wife and child at home waiting for him to bring in the rich, shiny ore.

The late summer morning broke still and warm, silent streaks of golden sun gilding the coarse rocks and dry brush of the camp area beside his cabin. This place, this hill that was to be their home as well as their livelihood, pleased him. The sight of the sun covering the common and ugly shapes of the stunted trees and rocks held a special glory. A glory to fit the dream they had held together . . . he, Mary Rose, and the little one.

Briley could still see the child, a tumbling, laughing five-year-old full of mischief and sweetness. She had wanted a pony and he kept putting her off saying they had no money. But they would have money someday he assured her . . . they would.

He began work in the long shaft inside the mine as soon as he had his coffee and sourdough biscuits. The shaft crawled over one hundred yards into the side of the mountain. Streaks of silver, varying from one to six inches wide and sometimes three inches deep, traveled this distance.

The entrance to the mine was behind a sledge of rock and covered by living vines. No one could see it as close as two feet away. His cabin was around the other side to discourage wanderers finding the mine opening.

Briley used a hammer and iron chisel steadily for three hours, breaking off fist-size hunks of the ore. Later he would sit and split the rocks, pulverizing the ore until he had extracted pieces carrying a high assay of pure silver.

He stopped at the height of the summer sun and made himself a meal of sliced dried venison and cold biscuits. He reheated his coffee.

The sun beat down on the pasture of the pole corral that held Asa, his burro, and the dark grulla mustang gelding he'd captured eight years ago. Briley carried a bucket of water from his shallow pool and watered the animals.

Asa came stolidly to her master and he patted her greying head with the tips of his fingers, then went back to the mine.

It was cooler in the mine, but by the end of the day he was sweat-soaked and dragging tired. Good tired. It was the only way to stifle the loneliness.

Briley had a pot of stew bubbling over hot coals. He had cut chunks of smoke-dry beef into onions and potatoes and simmered it all afternoon.

He bathed in a nearby shallow creek and hanged up his shirt to dry during the night.

Asa joined him by the fire. The small burro nuzzled industriously through the camp as she did every evening, unearthing hidden chunks of corncob or bits of piloncillos, the brown sugar cones she loved. The final tidbit was always in Briley's hip pocket. He laughed as she pushed him over and he was forced to dig the sugar out and hand it to her.

By the last flicker of the fire he opened a worn Bible and took out a photograph. It was dirty and broken across the middle. He stared for a long while, aching to touch the precious faces.

Another paper, equally yellow, he glanced at briefly. It read: Reward for capture of Jess Kendall; wanted for the shooting-murder of Ruff Whelper; signed Marshall Drew Pike, Wyoming Territory, 1860. Stiff from hard work, Briley bedded down under the stars and was soon asleep.

Chapter Five

Ed Lowery greeted Wash with, "Howdy." Then stood back to admire the stallion.

Ed Lowery was a life-long hostler and knew good horseflesh. But this horse was a cause to shake his head at. "One of them thoribreds, ain't it, Mister?" he concluded as he attempted to lay a hand on the horse's rump. Hoshaba snorted his displeasure and stepped aside.

"Yes, and rather edgy I'm afraid," Wash added. "I may have to rub him down myself."

"Not with Smoke Rising around, you won't. Thet's one hand what don't have no troubles makin' acquaintance of flighty critters. You'll see." He called out for his stable hand in a loud voice.

Smoke Rising was a small, trim figure dressed in the oldest pair of britches and scuffed boots Wash had ever seen. The pants were tight and fitted over a tiny waist and softly-rounded hips . . . the faded flannel shirt, missing its top button, only emphasized the fullness of the girl's figure.

Her dark blue eyes sparked when she saw Hoshaba. She did not even glance at Wash.

"Treat this'n special, Smoke," Ed Lowery said. "And put him in the last stall nex' to your mare."

He turned to Wash. "That little mustang mare o' hers is a sweet thang. She'll gentle him down right quick."

The girl glided sideways, putting her head near Hoshaba's shoulder. She murmured low, sing-song love words and raised her hand near his muzzle. He sniffed and blinked at her before edging back. But not much.

Wash watched, interested in her technique. He had developed his own way of handling skittish broncs and he liked what he saw her doing.

For several minutes she stayed beside the stallion, letting him nuzzle her shirted arm, her shoulder, and finally her back. Wash chuckled under his breath.

Then the girl walked toward the rear of the barn, turned back to Hoshaba and held out her hand. This time it mysteriously held a fistful of grain.

Hoshaba stretched out his neck. Sniffed. She moved further back. He wiggled his lips, sniffed again, stretched further. She walked to the stall door and stopped. Hoshaba snorted, pawed the ground . . . and followed her inside.

"She has a way all right." Wash lifted astonished eyebrows.

"Ain't never been no horse thet little girl didn't cotton to. She'll take fine care of thet one. My, he is a hummer."

"Isn't it a bit unusual for a young lady to be working as a stable hand?" Wash asked as they settled on a pay arrangement.

"Huh," Lowery lowered his voice and leaned close. "Spose so. But then she's lucky to git thet, the way folk feels. She come in to Granite Canyon three year ago carrying nothin' but an extra pair of moccasins and ridin' a Indian mustang pony. Folk took her for one of the Indian children. Wouldn't have nothin' to do with her.

"I took her in, jist to give her a bed. Then she bleached out and by gum, she was no Indian. Anyhows, she set to, fooling with the stock til purty soon she was doing all the work, scrubbin', feedin', and care in general. Pleased her, to do it, I guess. And too, no one ever offered to give her more lady-like work. She's growed into a mighty big help."

Wash strode back to the stall and watched as she rubbed the sleek, red coat of the powerful stallion. She could still be taken for an Indian he thought. Her hair, long and black, was plaited and her arms and face were sun-brown. But more than that there was a reserve about her that was not like a white woman.

She worked swiftly, but with pleasure and a definite smile of admiration for the horse.

"I'll come by and exercise him myself tomorrow," Wash informed her. She stopped, straightening to her full five feet, three inches. She looked at him for the first time, as if astonished that he would intrude.

"Of course, Mr.. . . ."

"Buchanan. I'm Wash Buchanan," he said.

"Mr. Buchanan," she acknowledged stiffly. "Anytime."

He grinned. She was a haughty one.

Wash sent for his trunks then took a room at the Trail End, overlooking Main Street. Two dollars a day they told him covered a real "tub" bath. He paid.

After the first bath he'd had in a week, he put on clean shirt and pants and adjusted his moneybelt. The leather pouch held over a thousand dollars in paper. He had converted the gold coins in that jar of Jake's into bonds for easier carrying.

He found the sheriff's office open.

A pasty-faced, barrel-chested man wearing a badge looked up from his desk. He took a breath and wheezed as he asked, "Can I help you?"

"I'm Wash Buchanan from St. Louis," Wash replied, glancing at the gun cabinet behind the sheriff. It was locked but through the glass he could see rifles and shotguns and a long row of handguns. A sense of unease hit him. He shuddered to think how many men this arsenal alone could kill. How many ordinary citizens have their own guns? He wondered.

"You the smart scout what made trouble for Jack?"

Wash removed his hat and rubbed his fingers through his hair. "Suppose so, if you call trouble wanting my horse away from cattle horns and stamping hooves."

The man leaned back in his chair. "I'm Sheriff Elias Miles, Mr. Buchanan, and I 'magine you're looking for your grandpa's place."

"Yes. And would you know who's handling his will?"

Elias Miles plopped a horehound into his mouth and wheezed so violently Wash thought he'd have to send for a doctor. Finally the man spoke. "That's being held by Mr. Simmons three doors down. He'll also tell you how to find the place."

Wash nodded and reached for the door. "Buchanan," the sheriff called. "Might be best if you sold the land soon's possible."

"Thanks," Wash said and walked out to find 'three doors down'.

Earnest Simmons Esquire greeted Wash with a death-gripping handshake. "Hello, hello, Washington. I'm happy you're here. Did you get my telegram?" Simmons was small and thin with long whiskers covering a caved-in chest.

"No," said Wash. "In fact I just found out today that my grandfather is dead. Could you tell me where his place is and let me see the will. I understand you hold it."

"Surely, surely," Earnest Simmons scooted to a desk and lifted a document off the top. Had he been reading it? Wash wondered. "Here is the will and as you can see it is very simple. He left the entire piece of land, 2423 acres, to you. He was so excited to know he had a grandson."

"You knew him?"

"Oh, not really. Your grandfather was very private. He rarely came to town. But the day he changed his will he bought a wagon load of lumber and tools and food. He had plans, he said, to fix up the house."

Wash wondered suddenly what the old man had looked like. His mother had only told him that he was tall and whip-cord strong. Earnest Simmons laid a paper on the desk and handed Wash a pen. "If you'll sign here I'll record the deed as transferred. I'm the resident clerk for the court."

Wash read the document. It looked okay and he signed. "You now own over 2000 acres of choice land," Simmons declared. He fingered his long beard and added, "Washington, I have been instructed to ask if you would sell your land. There is a ready buyer who'll pay a premium."

Wash frowned. "No sir. I'm anxious to use the land myself as a matter of fact. Who. . . ."

"I'm not at liberty to say who is interested but if you should change your mind, let me know. Now, it's too late to ride out to the place today. Would tomorrow after lunch be suitable?"

"Sure." Wash nodded.

"Then come by and my man, Frank, will take you out."

Outside Belle's Hats, Elizabeth Drennan greeted Wash warmly.

"A lovely chapeau, Miss Drennan," he complimented.

"Oh, please, call me Elizabeth. After all, if Dad and I are to be your host and hostess tomorrow night we'd best be on a first name basis." Her soft green eyes fairly glowed under the white straw hat.

"If that's an invitation then I accept," Wash countered.

A matched pair of blacks pulling a sleek black buggy drew up and J. T. Drennan reached down to shake hands. "Found your grandfather's land yet, boy?"

"Yes, I have. Or at least I know where it is. I'll see it tomorrow."

"Good. I hope our telling about his death didn't distress you too greatly. I like to see a man take hold the way you're doing. This will be an up-and-coming place one day. I've just been over to talk to the sheriff. He says my business is exactly what's needed to stop this 'cattle exchanging' we're having."

"Rustling?" Wash asked. "How bad is it?"

"Well, he didn't name names. And not many are reporting it. But it's simply a well-known fact, whether everyone reports it or not. But don't worry, we'll get you fixed up with a triple string of my finest wire, guaranteed to stop a surging stampede."

Elizabeth slipped her cool hand into Wash's and he automatically bowed as the buggy pulled away.

The sun was falling behind the buildings on main street. Wash could smell honeysuckle. A pleasant town, he thought. And it might indeed be an 'up-an-coming place.' But he wasn't thinking of barbed wire, he was remembering Elizabeth Drennan's smile.

Chapter Six

Near the Drovers, Wash picked up another smell . . . yeast-rising bread. He hadn't tasted that in years. He and Jake had feasted solely on biscuits and cornbread.

He went inside.

The Drovers saloon offered a drink on one side of the room and a pot of stew on the other. Tables in the center kept men playing cards and cradling bottles. A long bar was to the right. Languid, dusty "drovers" leaned on it.

On the far left a mammoth stone fireplace filled the whole wall and in it, a spit turned, dripping brown venison juice.

Then Wash recognized four of the men at the bar and his stomach tightened. Whelper and his three friends. Stoop-shoulder eyed him and immediately punched Jack.

Wash ignored them and took a table.

He ordered stew and a loaf of the hot bread from a kid with a greasy apron. As he supped coffee he saw a familiar form about to slip out the side entrance with a tray of food.

He caught up with her. "Miss!" he said. Smoke Rising turned and waited, but her gaze flew to the men at the bar. Wash spoke quietly. "I'd like to talk to you if you have a minute. About Hoshaba's feed."

"I was going to have supper, Mr. Buchanan. But I'll listen." She held the tray tightly and spoke in a low voice.

"Will you join me then. I was about to eat too."

"I don't eat here Mr. Buchanan," she stated flatly.

"Well, would you this once? I'd be obliged." He pulled out a chair and, taking her tray, placed it on the table. Her head lifted and she bit her bottom lip in a half-smile.

The four men moved as a group toward the fireplace.

Whelper wore a coat that flared at the sides to expose that bone-handled cannon he'd pointed at Wash. The man stood ram-rod stiff, his shoulders defiant. He stared at Smoke Rising with a glare that put goose bumps on Wash's neck. What did the man have to do with her?

Wash eased himself into his chair and watched Jack Whelper reach into a pocket and slowly pull out a Long Nine. Wash knew these were long thin cigars shipped from New England. Probably expensive way out here.

Biting the end off his cigar, Whelper flicked it into the fire. He began to chew, spit, and finally say, "We don't allow squaw-help to eat in the dining room in this town, Mr. Buchanan." His tone was condescending, somehow vulgar.

A hush fell on the room. No one spoke. Cards were

not shuffled. The silent stare of every man was on Smoke Rising.

"We think you'll find it better on the digestion if you will eat alone," Jack Whelper continued. Brute picked his teeth. Lewis sneered. Stoop-shoulder fondled an iron poker from the grate, grinning as he rubbed his hand along its sides.

Smoke Rising started to push back her chair but Wash caught her arm. His words sounded gracious and polite, yet they were said with an unmistakable threat. "On the contrary, she would delight the table of any gentleman." He put his hand over hers, holding her still.

"And I intend to enjoy the lady's company."

Lewis put his hand inside his coat. Did he have a hidden gun? Wash wondered. Would any of them actually draw on him in the saloon?

The barman coughed, slammed down a glass and hurried over to stand in front of Whelper. "Now, Lewis . . . Jack," he pleaded with his hands nervously wiping up and down his apron. "I can't afford another bust-up in my place. "He's new and . . . well, he'll come 'round, Jack."

Wash edged his chair to one side, his eye first on one and then on the other of the four. His muscles tensed and his knuckles turned white.

The barman began to plead again. Suddenly Jack Whelper whirled to nod angrily but reassuringly at the shaking barman. "Okay, Clem. Okay." Then he glanced at Smoke Rising as if he could stomp her into the earth. "Next time," he said, and stalked out of the saloon.

"You shouldn't have done that," Smoke Rising said. She pulled her hand from Wash's grip and nervously rearranged her plate of stew and coffee. "Jack Whelper won't let it pass. He'll be after you. You'd do well to take their advice. You don't really want to eat with me anyway."

"Why not?"

Wash studied her face. Looking at her eased the rapid beat of his pulse. Jack Whelper did not mean a thing.

"I like your looks, your company, and besides, I need to talk business." His stew came and he set to eating with relish, ignoring the looks from other tables. "Working in the livery is nothing to be ashamed of. Any work is something to be proud of. And the way you handle those horses!"

"It's not just my job, Mr. Buchanan, that causes the trouble. It's me. I'm what you call low-born. I'm not one of the fancy ladies such as you're used to. They call me 'squaw-woman.' "

"I'm glad you're not a fancy lady," he said, then added, " 'A brave and generous disposition like thine hath a value independent of condition and birth.' "

He winked as he dug his knife into a tub of butter. He lathered it onto half the loaf of bread and began eating as if he were starved.

"Are those your words?" she asked.

"No," he laughed. "But they're true. A brave knight once said them in a book. Do you read, Smoke Rising?"

She shook her head, then quickly told him. "I think I know how you want Hoshaba fed." She punched her stew meet with a fork, throwing a furtive glance at the door. "Oats and corn once a day with good dry hay at all times. Fresh water at his pleasure except after a workout when he needs to be given half gallons at hour intervals until he cools off."

"Right." Wash gulped the hot sugarless coffee. "Where did you come by a name like Smoke Rising?"

She hesitated. Then evidently deciding his question was sincere she replied, "Indians have a way of naming their people by things that happen or that are associated with them. When I first came to the Cheyenne camp the wind was blowing cold. It was from the north. As soon as they carried me into a tent the wind ceased and the smoke from their fires rose straight up . . . and winter was past. So my name is their way of remembering."

"You brought them luck," Wash added.

"Not really. The government began to harass them, trying to drive them to the reservation. The Great Chief Black Kettle made a bargain for peace which was not kept. The government men demanded the People live on land they would give them. For the years I was with my Cheyenne family we fled from one miserable place to another. Until I was fourteen when I either went with them to the reservation, or found my own way."

"It hasn't been easy, has it?" he asked matter-of-factly.

"No," she muttered and began to eat in silence.

Later, he walked her to her room behind the Livery and he was in his hotel by midnight.

Lights were scarce in the town, there were many dark alleys and shadowy storefronts. Men still drinking in the saloon were playing cards at a steady, night-eating pace. Wash decided to sleep in his moneybelt. One more night and he'd either keep the money at the ranch or put it in the bank.

What a day! He was achingly tired and despite the uncomfortable straw bed, he fell asleep quickly.

He never heard the handle of his door turn. He never

heard three booted figures hover for an instant, locating their target then lunge inside to envelop him in battle.

But the instant he was touched he reacted with the same full awareness he always did during those times of stress when he was tending sick horses.

He made a half-roll, jack-knifed his feet under him and careened to one side, forcing Brute's iron-fisted blow to miss and hit the bed frame.

Violent curses exploded from the man. The next blow paid for his miss. It caught Wash on the side of his head setting lights ablaze behind his eyes.

Then Brute was joined by the other two. They booted and twisted and knocked with malicious glee. Sometimes all at once.

Brute was not satisfied. He yanked Wash upright, hissing and spitting, shaking him like a rag doll. Lewis snorted and began pummeling with his soft pudgy fists.

Wash tumbled to the floor and rolled into a ball where Stoop-shoulder kicked his side and back until Wash slid into the dark black hole of unconsciousness.

Grunting like a dog, Lewis slipped a long skinny knife under Wash's moneybelt and split the leather apart. It rubbed the flesh raw as he pulled it off by one end and laughed. "Now leave town or the next time we'll take more than your money," he whispered.

Wash Buchanan did not hear it.

Chapter Seven

Asa stood with a drooping head as Briley heaved the pack on to her back and fastened it with a rope.

"Now girl, you know you wouldn't miss a trip to Cheyenne for all the tea in Chinie." He turned his head to spit tobacco juice onto a cactus curled brown long ago from other days of packing.

The grulla was saddled and Briley swung to after checking the Winchester and shoving it into the boot. He'd already buckled on his sidearm. The rifle was the only weapon he kept handy while working the mine. On his yearly trip to the bank he wanted the six-gun.

Ten miles out of sight of his mountain his gaze began to backtrack as often as scout ahead. He felt his hackles rise. "And you know what that means, Asa," he mumbled.

Maybe this was the day. Maybe after all these years they were finally closing in on him. Maybe they'd just now found out about him, who he really was, and been waiting for him to surface. Well, he wouldn't be taken easily.

Heat waves danced off the pack on the burro's back as they reached the middle of a barren plain. The grass was stubby and dead and the grulla mustang stirred up dust devils with his plodding hooves.

A wry grin lifted the corners of Briley's tobacco-stained lips. Fifteen years had not done away with the gnawing fear of being hunted. He steadied himself in the saddle, eased the Winchester out of the boot. He let Asa fall behind so that he could watch their rear without seeming to.

There! Behind the mesquite grove he had just circled, a bush moved. How many would there be?

Sweat dripped off his chin. He craved a drink but didn't dare. A swish of dove wings fluttered up from the ground ahead of the bush. They were following close.

Briley concentrated on getting Asa over the first rocky incline that led through the hills called McKitchen Pass. He avoided the usual low-lying trail and deliberately led the complaining burro up a steeper path that wound into a high-walled pocket. It formed a natural room surrounded by red rock walls.

The sun was fierce in the center, but along the edges of the circle the air was cool and he stopped in a spot of shade.

He knew they could not see him now. They had taken the short way and would realize what he had done only after they'd gone some distance.

He dismounted and dropped the reins. The pack was unusually heavy and Briley let it drop where he stood. His plan made, he felt no panic.

In one of the natural crannies—a place between the

hillside and a dislodgement of rock boulders—he dragged the ore. The sack fitted easily into a niche inside the crack and he cut a few tumbleweed bushes and crammed them on top. Not really enough to completely hide his treasure.

Asa's ears tweaked. She lifted her head. Horses' hooves were striking rock on the far side of the pass. Briley paid no attention but guided Asa out of the cul-de-sac. Outside, he slung the sweat from his face with a swift and efficient finger. He poured Asa and the grulla a drink from his canteen.

As he pulled onto the regular trail he held a steady pace for the next ten minutes, then turned off abruptly and tied Asa under a grove of trees. He ground-reined the grulla.

Taking the rifle he climbed the ridge and circled back to his rear—skirting the path he had just made.

He climbed atop the very hill where he had hidden the pack. He could see without being seen.

They were there. Two men were dragging the ore out of the niche. Maybe they wanted the silver more than they wanted him. Were they really after him? Or just the ore?

Briley raised the Winchester and blew dust at the boot tips of the one closest.

The men dropped the sack, their hands flew up at the same time and they whirled to face the direction of the bullet.

"You lookin' for me, boys?" Briley punctured the still air with a booming voice. The old stultifying fear always left him when the showdown came.

"Fraid I'm the rightful—lawful—owner of that ore

rock, gents. An if you're plannin' to take me in as well . . . then you've got double trouble."

The bigger man threw a puzzled glance at his companion. He let his eye rove along the ridge behind Briley, evidently searching for an accomplice.

"Drop your guns," Briley said in a friendly way.

"Yea, sure," the robbers replied at the same time.

Instead of dropping their guns, they fell to the ground, rolled apart, and came up firing. They unloaded several rapid shots then dived for the shelter of the overhanging ridge.

"Darn!" muttered Briley and he grabbed his left arm. They nicked him. They were either mighty smart robbers, or part of a posse that wanted extra pay along with the grab. Whichever, he would need to move fast and careful.

"I didn't put that ore in that particlar place fer nothin'," Briley mumbled as he slid off his perch. He landed at the bottom of the ridge with a jar that shook him all over. He felt the blood ooze from his arm but it wasn't pulsing. It would be okay.

Moving faster than he had in years, he snaked around the hill to a place on the far side. Bushes covered a narrow crevasse but he pushed his way in. He would come out ahead of the men and opposite the overhang.

He treaded easy through the last feet of the crack. He didn't want them to hear him.

When he saw daylight at the end of the narrow tunnel he stopped. One more foot and he'd have a clear shot at the men huddled under the overhang in that circled canyon room.

Briley's head ached. His finger was damp on the trigger. He'd never killed a man. Despite what they said, despite what old Ruff Whelper had claimed, Briley had never shot a man.

He stepped out into the bright sun. The two men were standing with their back to him, guns in hand.

Briley coughed. He'd not shoot in the back.

They turned, raised their rifles and fired.

The hastily fired rifle slugs tore into the soft red sandstone over Briley's head. A rockchip ricocheted, scarring his cheek.

Briley held an ancient Dragoon Colt .45 he'd bought during the war. The handgun had put many a rabbit in the stew-pot for him and despite its age he knew it was a wiser choice than a rifle to down a man at close range.

The hammer was back and his slippery trigger finger never hesitated. It jerked, pumping two bullets each into the chests of the would-be robbers.

Briley took a long deep breath then walked over and toed the first man. He was already dead. The second groaned and Briley stooped down. "You two after me or my gold?" he demanded.

The man gurgled, blood drooling out of the side of his mouth. "You? Wh . . . why we want you?" his voice choked. But he needed to talk. He had to say, "We wa . . . wanted us a good time fer once . . . an . . . And. . . ." He stopped to cough then ended, "We near 'bout had it, didn't we. . . ."

Briley stood, letting the .45 drop to his side. "If I'd a knowed I'd a given you a good time. Darn! Shoulda' knowed you was only two-bit robbers . . . not no goldurned posse men."

Chapter Eight

Wash Buchanan woke in the early dark hours of the morning. A splitting headache drove him to douse his head under a pitcher of water. He poured a glass of water and drank. He finished it and poured another.

What happened? Why did he feel like a twice-thrown bronc rider? He touched his face and winced. When he glanced into the fly-specked mirror he groaned. His right eye was blood red. He could not see straight. And he couldn't remember. . . . Yes, it came to him. Whelper's men.

His stomach suddenly doing flipflops, he grabbed at his waist. Gone! All the money Jake and he had saved for the last ten years swiped in a five minute brawl.

He staggered to the bed, fell across it, and slept.

He wakened to a raging thirst. He put a hand to his back and tried to sit up. Pain stabbed through his body like a knife.

He rested, panting for strength. In thirty minutes he

tried again. This time he sat up. He sat for another long spell then pulled himself upright.

His shirt had been ripped apart, his chest underneath was turning blue. He hoped no ribs were broken. In the mirror he saw that his bloody eye was now closed.

Wash's mind was in a whirl. He was to meet Simmons's man to ride out to the land. Would he ever make it?

In the hall the pickup boy was about to go downstairs. "Hey, boy," Wash called. "Bring me a pot of coffee will you? And whatever food you can find."

The boy stared, then fled.

He was soon back with the coffee and a pot of soup. "Ma says this will fix you up. And a cold rag on the sore places never fails. You in a fight, Mister?"

Wash nodded, accepting the hot coffee with trembling hands. "Thank her for me, kid. I . . . I don't have any money right now."

"That's okay. It's what I git paid to do." He quietly slipped away.

The coffee eased the headache and sure enough, a damp rag held over the bruised eye worked wonders. After another rest period he drank the soup and felt as if he would be able to ride.

But first he wanted to see the sheriff.

Elias Miles did a double-take as soon as Wash walked in. The sheriff reached for a horehound and was barely able to wheeze, "What happened?"

"I think you know. Just didn't realize how bad a bust-up they'd give me, did you?" This was risky. But Wash figured the good sheriff was buddy to anything Whelper wanted. Nevertheless, he needed to report his missing money.

"I'd like to file charges against the men who did this. I recognized them. Jack Whelper's brother and those two sidekicks of his. And they took my money."

Miles sat down. He seemed to need a minute to think. "You say it was the Whelpers? Let's see now . . . You couldn't really recognize faces in a dark room at night, could you? And those boys were in the Drovers till midnight when I myself saw them ride for home." He concluded with a satisfied nod.

Then he started again. "You understand, Buchanan, the Whelpers are old family here. Maybe they're a mite quick tempered, but Jack is on our city council."

Sheriff Miles shuffled papers on his desk and added, "Be no need to bring them in. I will keep a lookout for the money, however, in case someone tries to spend it 'round town. You identify it?"

"Yes," he said sadly. "They were bearer bonds."

Wash set his hat firmly over the cut on his forehead. Then he had a thought. "Sheriff, who would come into ownership of my grandfather's place if I were to leave and never take possession of it?"

Elias Miles blanched but he replied as if he had been thinking of it already, "After seven years it would be 'squatter's rights' land . . . whoever was living on it and using it could claim it."

"And if I were dead?"

Miles' lungs swelled then let go a wheezing reply. "It would become open range."

A scalding sun seared the weeds to a golden brown beside the livery. Inside, the horses stood in the dark, cooler recesses of the stalls with heads down.

A loud piercing whistle welcomed Wash. He pressed

his swollen face against the cool neck of Hoshaba. At least you're all right, he thought.

Smoke Rising's rangy, short-eared mare in the next stall poked her head over the siding and nuzzled Hoshaba's rump. Wash laughed. "You like him too, huh?" He brushed back her coarse mane, studying her confirmation.

"She has no breeding, Mr. Buchanan. She's one of the wild mustangs that roam the valleys in the land of the Cheyenne."

When Wash looked up, Smoke Rising gasped. The water in the bucket she carried sloshed so fiercely she was forced to set it down.

"I warned you," she whispered to herself.

The girl wore a different shirt, one not as tight and not missing a button. But it was a man's shirt. Lowery's cast-off? Her hair was freshly washed, still damp, hanging loose down her back. Wash caught a whiff of sage or some other herb's scent.

"I knew Jack would not take what you did. I . . . I'm sorry. Please do not talk to me again."

"Why are you afraid of Jack Whelper, Smoke Rising?"

She buried her forehead in the mare's shoulder. A shudder convulsed her body. "He wants me to be . . . to be his girl. And I won't. My skin crawls when I'm in his presence."

Her head lifted stubbornly. "I'm no lady, Mr. Buchanan, but neither will I let the likes of that man touch me. I will not become his property simply because of my up-bringing."

Wash was surprised at her candor. "Good. And you shouldn't. But as to your up-bringing, you're no different from the rest of us."

"Yes. Yes I am. I am not only an abandoned waif, I am the white child of the Cheyenne. I may as well be Cheyenne." Her words were bitter.

"Your English is perfect. How is that?"

"One of the women had been taught by a priest. She spoke to me in English from the first. She also sheltered me from Joe Little Horn who wanted to take me for his woman.

"Now I ask *you.* They say you are Washington Marion Buchanan. Are you a son of Francis Marion Ross who lives in the hills north of Granite?"

"A grandson. My mother named me Marion, but she refused to add the Francis to it. Instead she gave me another war hero's name, Washington. It seems my grandfather warned her against the name Francis Marion even before she married. 'You have two girls' names,' he was always teased."

Wash hunched his shoulders, "But the name is an honored one and I wouldn't have minded it. Francis Marion fought the British from out of the bayous of South Carolina. He was so successful they dubbed him The Swamp Fox. This was during the Revolution . . . you know the great war America waged to be free from England?"

"I have heard of it."

"Anyway, my great great grandfather fought with him. And named his son after him, and he named *his* son after him."

Smoke Rising made a motion with her hand Wash did not understand. "It is good," she said, "to be such a part of the People."

"Did you know my grandfather?"

"No. But I have ridden many times over his land. There are manadas in the breaks near the west buttes. I often go there to think of my other life . . . and how it was."

"Manadas?"

"Bands of mustangs."

Wash nodded toward the mare. "What have you named her? And how did you come to have her?"

"I call her Sister," Smoke Rising said and smiled secretly. "She was given to me by Joe Little Horn. And she *is* my sister."

Wash put a halter on Hoshaba and led him into the aisle. Smoke Rising cupped her hand under the horse's velvet nose. She lowered her face until her own nose touched his. She closed her eyes and breathed as one with the stallion. Slowly she pulled away. She said, "He is sacred, Washington Marion Buchanan. Be careful, he is one of the gods."

Wash froze. What did she mean? He wanted her to explain it but she busied herself with the water bucket and he could not bring himself to ask her.

As he pulled his saddle off the stall rail he flinched. His side hurt like heck.

Smoke Rising looked over, took the lightweight riding saddle from him, tossed it on Hoshaba and buckled the girth.

Wash eased gently aboard and reined out the doors.

Chapter Nine

For the first mile, the sway and bump of the horse was agony. But the sun and constant movement soon worked into his muscles and Wash felt less pain. He even began to enjoy the scenery.

The memory of his lost money nagged at the edge of his mind. Although he had no idea how, he intended to get it back.

The Ross ranch was ten miles northeast of Granite. The land began just south of the Horse Creek river. It was bordered by it on two sides, and rose off good pasture to the timber along Diamond Peak. An awesome accumulation of boulders and ridges split the southwest part into a region of smaller valleys and creeks and ended in Wild Horse Gorge.

"We'll see the Gorge up ahead," Frank Potter barked as he reined his horse toward a long flat prairie covered with short grama grass. Potter was a rough, wind-blistered cowhand who knew every stitch of the country.

"Wild Horse Gorge?" Wash asked and let Hoshaba's head drop to munch the delectable green. The thoroughbred had been difficult to keep in line with Potter's mount. He wanted to race. The clear open air inflamed him and he constantly fought the bit.

"Yes, that's what it's called. The Cheyenne and Arapaho Indians used this field to catch bands of mustangs. They roam the valleys among the Yellow Cat Buttes. The Indians would drive them here where no stallion dared lead his mares over that drop. Look for yourself."

Wash sat on Hoshaba not ten feet from the edge of a sheer cliff that dropped suddenly off the prairie. The chasm went straight down, cutting through the earth as far as he could see. Hoshaba pranced nearer, glanced into the pit and with a convulsive shiver, began backing away.

"See," Potter declared. "He knows the danger. To your right, this side of that lone clump of trees, is the only place narrow enough for a possible jump. But so far no horse has ever tried it and lived.

"Come on, we'll ride to the house."

Wash was not prepared for it. A ragged track overgrown with weeds led to a broken-down fence. Inside the yard stood a battered wagon, one wheel off. The few corrals were small with gates falling off their hinges. And when he looked at the house tears welled in his eyes.

Unpainted . . . maybe two rooms . . . windows smashed and covered over with tar paper . . . the chimney leaning to one side. Never had a porch been built, or a flower or a tree been lovingly planted to make the place a home.

"Granpa," Wash muttered, "No wonder you didn't

want your only daughter to leave. You were so alone. I'm sorry. You were alone all those years and we never knew it."

"Are there any cattle?" he finally managed in a choked voice when Potter pulled up beside him.

"Years ago it was thought Ross ran a thousand or so, using the mountain meadows and draws. And I know personal he had several hundred up until his death."

"Where is he buried?"

"Sheriff Miles told me he and his men put your granpa on that hill." He pointed.

Wash dismounted and walked up the small incline. There was a pile of grey stones under a scrub oak. No flowers had been put on it. No marker.

Wash toed one of the stones back into place, then suddenly realizing he did not know how the old man died he asked, "Potter, How did he die? What killed my grandfather?"

Potter squinted, took out a large red handkerchief and mopped his brow. "Why, he was killed right there by the wagon, the one he'd just bought all those goods in. The Sheriff said they found him with a bullet hole right in the middle of his chest.

"Thought you knew."

While Wash shaved the next morning a note was pushed under his door. *"We know about your trouble. But if you feel up to it, meet us tonight at Delmonico's. Elizabeth and J. T."*

Maybe a good steak would make him feel better. Right now he felt as if that twice-throwed bronc rider in the mirror might've been "thrice-throwed."

Finding out his grandfather had been killed hadn't helped.

Who would want to murder a lonely, helpless old man? Wash wondered. Could it be Jack Whelper again? Was there some connection with his grandfather . . . or the ranch . . . that added to Whelper's being so riled up at himself?

He'd ask around. He needed to know more.

He confronted Sheriff Miles outside the Drovers. "Why didn't you tell me my grandfather had been shot," he demanded, anger rising in his throat like hot bile.

Elias Miles glanced around, then edged to one side of the Drovers' swinging door. "Look, Buchanan. There's no way we can know who shot your granpa. It rained heavy right after, so's there was no tracks. And there was no reason. . . ."

"That's right, Sheriff," Wash growled. "There was no reason for anyone to shoot a harmless old man."

"Sorry. . . ." Rattled into a hard wheeze, Miles backed quickly into the saloon.

Wash swiped a hand through his hair and walked down to Earnest Simmons's office. He asked the startled man the same question he'd asked the sheriff.

"Why, I thought you knew." Simmons clasped his fingers together and frowned.

Wash took a deep breath. It would do no good to badger the whole town. He sat down in the chair across from Simmons and said, "Mr. Simmons, I need to know where I stand. Tell me about Jack Whelper."

Simmons removed his spectacles and pressed a finger into his eyes. When he looked up his lips tightened. "I should've mentioned it before but you understand a killing out here does not mean the same thing it does back east . . . where you come from. Here we have our own code of law. And sometimes that code is simply who's the biggest and fastest and . . . well, the sneakiest."

"You're saying nothing will be done about it?"

"That's correct."

Wash pounded his fist against the chair arm. "Then tell me something about these Whelpers."

Simmons nodded. "They buy and sell cattle. They have for the last five years. Before that, they sold only their own off the Winged W. That was when Lofton Whelper, the boys' uncle, was alive and running things. When he died, the place cut down on its own range cattle. But they still run enough of the W brand to keep top hands working. And to keep Jack Whelper in gambling money."

Wash waited for more.

Simmons cleared his throat, picked up a pen and thumped it on his desk. Finally he said, "The Winged W was a bustling place while Ruff Whelper was alive. Ruff was their father and . . . well, the trouble began when he was killed."

"What trouble?"

"Ruff owned a mercantile store. He had several hands running it while he spent time at the ranch. One night . . . no one knows how or why . . . Ruff came back to the store late, found his safe being robbed, and was shot by the robber. Before he died he told who the man was. One of his hands. A man by the name of Jess Kendall."

"Did they get this Jess Kendall?"

"No. He fled the country. Left a wife and five-year-old daughter behind."

"And he's never been caught?"

"The boys and their uncle Lofton put out warrants and reward money, even sent a posse after the man. They never caught him and finally, when Lofton died, the boys quit hunting."

"How long ago was the killing?"

"Fifteen . . . sixteen years."

"And the wife and daughter. Are they still around?"

"Oh, no. Rumor has it they both died of the ague soon after Kendall fled. Sorry bit of doings."

"One more question. Is there any reason you can think of why Jack Whelper would want to own my grandfather's spread? He was the one offering to buy it, right?"

Simmons looked out the small window beside his desk. "No, Washington. I don't know why he would want your spread."

"Thanks, Mr. Simmons." Wash stood and offered his hand.

Hesitantly, the little man took it but he added, "Don't get into this, son. Take your horse and live on your land. Or better, go back to St. Louis."

Wash shook his head. "Can't Mr. Simmons. Just can't."

Chapter Ten

Elizabeth wore a dark red gown. The neckline dipped daringly in front, reminding Wash of the St. Louis ladies he'd seen one night at the home of Joseph Brown. Wash had just delivered the mayor a new six-passenger rockaway pulled by two solid black geldings. One of the finest sets he and Jake had ever put together. He had lingered a moment to enjoy the glitter as the mayor's wife and daughters climbed aboard.

He was enjoying this more. Elizabeth Drennan outshined any of those elegant swanks.

But she wore a worried frown as he joined them at the table in Delmonico's. Wash pulled at his sleeve to cover the ugly cut on his wrist. He had no suit. He was wearing his white shirt and a black string tie, with grey pants and his regular soft leather riding boots. But it was not his clothes that worried Elizabeth. "Oh, Washington, how awful. Your . . . your face is cut, and that eye! Have you seen Doc Grover?"

"No, I'll be all right. Just take a few days."

The tables in the dining room of Delmonico's were draped with white clothes and set with crystal glasses. The muted lights reflected off a dazzling chandelier. Wash felt transported and a little homesick—sad that he might never have a taste of the city life again.

"Should have a hunk of that steak to put on your eye, boy," J. T. waved his glass of wine toward Wash. "They gave you a fair walloping. Along with stealing your money, I hear. Should have put it in the bank, you know. The banker is a nice man. Name of Parker.

"But don't worry, Buchanan. I'll see you get another roll to get started."

"No thanks, Mr. Drennan. You see, I intend to get my own money back."

Elizabeth's smile was quick. "I told father not to offer. But it may not be easy to get your money back, Wash. Rumor also has it you're accusing Jack Whelper and his brother. Is that true?" Her eyes glistened with concern.

"I *know* they did it," he stated.

"Just because of a tiff over the 'stable princess'?" Her voice teased.

Wash's grip tightened on the slender stem of his wine glass. "Rumor again?"

"Small town, Wash." She grinned.

"Now Elizabeth." J. T. shot Wash a knowing wink. "Don't worry about rivals yet, my dear. Give the man time."

Suddenly Elizabeth grew serious. She looked straight at Wash and said, "There's only one way to put yourself on equal terms with Jack Whelper, Washington."

He thought he knew what she would say.

"You don't wear a gun, do you?" She touched her mouth with the edge of a napkin.

"That's not my way, Elizabeth." He wanted to say why, that guns and shooting someone only left hurt and more pain. He didn't think she would understand.

"Think about it. If you stay out here you'll have to meet these shysters on their terms. Won't he dad? It's too dangerous not to be armed. I . . . I worry about that. Please, get yourself a gun."

She was reassuring, her argument straight-forward. Wash thought she was probably right. He hoped not.

They lingered late over coffee then Wash walked with them to their buggy. They could hear the tinny piano from The Drovers and Elizabeth smiled and began to hum. "We'll dance together sometime, Washington. When you're feeling up to it." She brushed his cheek with cool lips and climbed into the buggy.

Wash was tired but he knew he couldn't sleep. Maybe he'd watch a game of poker, help clear his mind.

The Drovers was raucus with the sound of the piano and lit bright as day. A group of young sun-burned cowboys lingered on the porch in front. They were all drunk. One was holding a bottle and singing an old Irish ballad in a really good tenor voice. Wash thought he'd like to hear him when he wasn't soused.

Two other hands argued about a girl in a gold dress. "She meant me," one declared. Wash leaned against a post and listened to another tell about the horse he'd busted "this very day." The young cowpoke was thin with a white forehead that had been protected by his hat. A long newly-made gash ran down one cheek. Now he stood on wobbly legs, telling his story with great earnestness. Wash smiled, realizing the boy was attacking the bronc-busting in the wrong way.

Suddenly a rider reined his horse in front of the cowboys and slowly climbed down. Glancing at the cowhands only for an instant, he started to tie his roan gelding to the rail. The young bronc-buster stopped in his speech-making and stared at the man and the horse. Wash felt uneasy, he sensed trouble.

"Whut'chu doin' with my horse?" the boy slurred and stepped toward the man. "That's my horse." He pointed as if that would settle the question. "I just broke 'im today. See this cut on my face? Got it fallin' off the devil." He turned to his friends for confirmation and got none.

Wash felt his pulse begin to beat faster. For some reason the other cowboys were not going to back up their friend. They began to pull away. Even the singer stopped singing when his buddy touched his arm.

"This is not your horse." The strange rider made his statement without a smile. He pushed past the boy who immediately grabbed his arm and cried, "Wait up. That's my horse I said."

A stout, older man stepped up and took the young man by the shoulder. "Don't Joey, that's not the roan you rode today. Come on, let's get another drink."

"No," the boy insisted, stumbling against the rail as he turned toward the stranger. Pushing his flat palm against the man's chest he waggled a finger. "You stole my horse!" he cried.

The stranger eased back, glaring at the kid. He was three feet from Wash and when Wash saw the man's eyes he knew it was too late.

The man made one more attempt to move past the

cowboy and when the irate youth touched him again he whirled, pulled a huge .45 Peacemaker and blew the young man back into the street.

The singer cried, "Oh, no, no, no!" The older man turned and ran toward the sheriff's office. Clem appeared white-faced in the doorway of his saloon.

The comrades of the gutted youth melted into the night. Wash watched the gunman walk past Clem into The Drovers. He couldn't believe what he'd just witnessed. The cold, no-reason killing of a kid. Who was this man?

Sheriff Miles came running, wheezing, his hand on the gun at his hip. He stopped to look down at the dead boy. He shook his head, then seeing Wash standing on the step he said quietly, "The man did this is Elliott 'Bull' Nettles and he's Whelper's new gun. You better leave town, Buchanan."

Wash knew the Whelper ranch was east of his grandfather's. He had studied the maps in Mr. Simmons's office so that when he came to a creek splitting north and east, he took the east fork. A deep-rutted path cut through the dead grass and he reined Hoshaba toward it.

The stabbing memory of his lost money caused him to kick the stallion into a trot. He had no plan to regain his goods and he did not know what to expect, he was driven by an urge he had never known, a desire to smash Jack Whelper in the face. And the bald brute . . . ah, how good it would feel to get his hands on that one.

They had guns. But—Wash shook his head—evidently not enough for Jack Whelper. He'd had to send for one more. Wash shuddered, remembering those "dead" eyes and the unbelievable speed of Bull Nettles as he shot the kid.

Confronting Whelper on his own spread was more than dangerous. Shooting a trespasser would be hailed by the sheriff as a smart thing. It would certainly fit in with this western idea of self justice.

The difference of this country and its way of individual law was churning in Wash like a storm. Coming from St. Louis where men walked the streets in freedom from thieves and robbers, where community law settled disputes, Wash felt helpless.

Hoshaba loped easily, lifting his quivering nostrils to the odor of bitter weed, flicking his head side to side to catch the movement of bug or snake along the trail. The hot dry air filled his great chest with power and he longed to run. But the tenseness of Wash on his back made him uncertain. He skirted a prairie dog hole then danced back into the dusty trailroad.

Wash kept an eye out for riders, hidden or otherwise. But they continued to travel unmolested. When he thought he must have taken the wrong split, he sighted a corral up ahead. The ranch house stood five hundred yards beyond it. He slowed Hoshaba to a walk. Funny, the corral looked unused, the shed next to it grown up in weeds. There was not work going on that he could see. Where were all those hands who worked for Whelper?

And where were the cattle?

Wash soon learned where the hands were.

One pointed a rifle from behind the wellhouse. Two guns were stationed atop the hayshed on his right. And at least three were lined up behind Jack Whelper and Lewis on the porch.

Somehow they had seen him coming.

Wash felt the hair stand up on the back of his neck. He nudged Hoshaba toward the steps. It was useless to run. He'd be gunned down before he could get to the corrals.

He'd try talking.

Wash straightened his aching back and patted the shivering flesh of Hoshaba's withers. The stallion snorted and Wash spoke to him low and easy. "Whoa, boy. We're just gonna visit awhile."

"I can see why you wanted to protect the horse, Buchanan," Jack Whelper said as he stepped off the porch. The man's mouth twitched at the sight of Hoshaba up close.

"What'll you take for him?"

Wash stared. Did the man want to buy everything he saw?

"Get down and sit. We'll talk *land* then, if you're not interested in horses." Whelper motioned to the chairs on the porch. The standing guard never moved. "I'll introduce you to my hands. This is my brother, Lewis, the big bald guy is Slick, and that's Stoop Ragan. I believe you've met them, but not formally."

Wash continued to sit quietly. What did Whelper mean by this "friendly" tactic? Fine, except all those ready guns said if a new approach didn't work, there was always the old one. And where was Nettles?

"You're right, Whelper," Wash uttered through gritted teeth. "I have met those three before. They beat me up and took my money. I want it back."

"Ah, son," Whelper sing-songed. "You can't prove that. Now why don't you let me give you two hundred for this horse here and you'll have enough for a ticket back to St. Louis."

"And leave the ranch my grandfather owned?" Wash glanced around at the armed men. If a fight started he'd be cut in half. How could he wiggle out of this?

While Jack Whelper lit one of his Long Nines and blew smoke haughtily into the air, Wash said, "But perhaps you can help me since we're neighbors. I understand my grandfather had cattle and yet I've seen none. As a matter of fact I didn't notice any grazing on your spread as I rode in. Where are the cattle, Whelper? Where do you find all the beeves you sell?"

Jack Whelper's face flooded dark with blood. He threw aside the cigar and stepped toward man and horse as if to grab Wash's leg. He stopped when the stallion threw up his head in warning.

Wash held his breath. The men on the porch raised their guns and Bull Nettles suddenly appeared from inside the doorway. He was at Whelper's elbow with the same lightning speed he'd used to draw on that boy. Wash knew now why he'd been sent for. Whelper wanted a personal body guard.

Muscles in Wash Buchanan's calves communicated a message to Hoshaba. The horse moved back, his hooves digging restlessly in the sand.

Whelper raised a staying hand to his crew. "Get off my land," was a snarl.

Wash should have gone then. But he couldn't let the thief have the last word. "This is not the end, Whelper. I intend to get my money back. You'd better keep your dogs handy."

He turned Hoshaba and raced down the trail, expecting

a bullet in the back at every lunge of the saddle. But no bullet came and he rode into Granite without stopping, letting the grind of the long run defuse his anger . . . and fear.

Chapter Eleven

Wash stepped into the big stallion's stall three days later just as the sun's rays seeped into the old livery barn. During those three days he had talked around, found the other men on that "town council" Sheriff Miles had mentioned, explained the robbery and beating. All three worthies had mumbled their concern and walked away.

Then he had sent a telegraph to the United States Marshall in Cheyenne. It might take a week or so for a response but Wash could think of no other way to go.

Wash stooped to finish the rubdown on Hoshaba's legs and heard: "He needs another workout, Mr. Buchanan." Smoke Rising finished tightening the girth under a small paint and tied it to a post, ready for its rider to claim.

"Hey," Wash said. "How about calling me Wash, and yes, he does. He gets edgy without a regular routine."

"Did you get your money back?" Smoke Rising crossed her arms like an angry mother.

Wash smiled. She didn't need to say I told you so.

"No," he said. Then he felt a cold shiver as he recalled Whelper's guns aimed at his back as he left the Whelper ranch. Darn! He was lucky to be alive.

But what he had said about not seeing cattle had banged Whelper's sore elbow. And it was stranger than ever about the cattle. Yesterday Whelper moved another hundred steers onto the rails headed for Fort Bridger. When Wash had asked Ed about it the hostler said Whelper had cattle, "All over." All over where? Wash wondered.

He tossed the saddle onto Hoshaba's back, this time without wincing. He seemed to be fully recovered from the beating.

Sister snorted when she saw Hoshaba walk by and Wash stopped. "Smoke Rising, you said the other day you often rode over my grandfather's land and that there were manadas near the buttes. Come show me."

The girl pushed back a lock of hair and said, "Must work."

"No you don't. I'll talk to Ed and I'll get a picnic lunch from the Trail End's kitchen. Please."

When he added the please her head flew up in astonishment. "You ask me please?"

"Yes. Please."

"No one has ever asked me please," she muttered. "Then yes, I will show you the wild horses."

An hour later Wash was back at the livery, a picnic lunch of meat pies and apples tucked away. As he and Smoke rode out the wide doors, the Drennan's buggy pulled alongside.

Elizabeth waved and flashed Wash her brilliant smile. "Hello," she said.

Wash nodded, reining Hoshaba tightly away from the

buggy wheels. The stallion danced and fidgeted, ready for his ride.

When Wash noticed Elizabeth staring at Smoke Rising, he asked, "Do you know each other? Elizabeth Drennan, Smoke Rising . . ." He hesitated, realizing he did not know another name for her.

"Pleased to meet you," Elizabeth said with a smile for Smoke Rising as brilliant as the one for Wash. She looked at him then and said, "We'll have to go riding sometime. I have a workhorse of a gelding that I'll stack against that red of yours." She laughed and pulled at the edges of her white leather gloves. "There's a dance Saturday night, Wash. We always have one after the summer round-ups. I'll save one for you."

With one swift movement Elizabeth reined the buggy around and trotted her team toward the bank.

"She is very beautiful," was Smoke Rising's comment as she kicked Sister onto the north trail.

Smoke Rising on Sister was a sight to behold. Wash could not take his eyes off them. The girl rode without a saddle, her bare legs dangling free. She used a halter, without a bit, keeping one arm raised to the heavens for balance. Together she and the rangy mare pranced and flitted beside Hoshaba until some secret urge happened upon them at once and they gave high-pitched whinnies and bounded across the prairie.

It was all Wash could do to catch them.

They rode directly north the ten miles to his land. Then cut northwest on a rutted trail that led them another mile to the ranch house where his grandfather had homesteaded. Wash was uneasy. He didn't particularly want to enter that wasted hull, but Smoke Rising slid off Sister and marched in the front door.

Wash took a breath and followed.

Rat droppings littered the floor. Spider webs shimmered in the sun that filtered through cracks in the walls. There was an open fireplace, a hand-sawn table with a bench. Whatever goods Francis Ross had purchased in town the day he changed his will were nowhere evident.

Old boots stood in one corner and a skillet and a few crockery plates sat forlornly on a shelf.

"Go," Smoke Rising whispered. Wash thought for a moment she meant for them to leave. Then he saw her nod at a door leading to the other room.

Wash pulled his hat off and with a toe, eased back the rickety door.

In one side of the large bedroom stood an iron bed with the sagging mattress and coverless pillow holding the indented shape of an old man. There was a stand with a pitcher and glass on it. Then Wash's glance flicked to the other side of the room. "Oh, my," he breathed. "Oh, my."

There stood a bed and a dresser with all the fineries a young woman living in the back-wilds of such a place might own.

The coverlet on the bed was dusty, but it had once been colorful, with flowers along the edge.

Wash tiptoed over to the dresser and picked up a mirror with a silver handle. Three odd little pieces of jewelry lay in a crystal bowl. There was a beautiful old lamp on another handsawn side table—this table was finely carved with leaf-cuts down the legs.

Wash could not believe it but this must have been the

sleeping side for his mother when she still lived with her father. And he had never changed it.

Gingerly, Wash opened one of the drawers in the chest. A pair of long cotton socks with holes, a scarf, evidently discarded . . . and a letter. His hand trembling, Wash picked up the letter. In the left corner was the return address and name: *Lily Buchanan, Chesterton Academy, Pulver Street, Philadelphia, Pennsylvania.* His mother, Lily Mae Ross Buchanan.

Wash's mouth went dry. In the ten years he had lived with his mother she'd never said anything about writing to her father.

He turned the soiled letter over. It had been opened. His grandfather had read it. Now Wash read it.

July 1852: Father. I hope this letter gets to you. I'm sending it with a friend who is traveling to Utah . . . over one of those wretched wagon train trails, the Overland I think they call it.

I hope you are well. John and I live at the Academy in a very pleasant cottage. John teaches history.

Father, if you could see and talk with John as he is here, you would know why I love him, why I had to go with him. Please, try and understand that I still love you, but my life could never be whole without John. Let me know you forgive me. Your daughter, Lily.

Wash put the ragged letter back into the envelope and shook his head. Granpa Ross, he thought to himself, stubborn old coot that you were, you did not answer.

That's why she never told me about writing to you. She was hurt and ashamed. What a waste you made of it all.

Standing in the doorway Smoke Rising asked, "Do you want to be alone?"

Wash squashed his hat onto his head and strode past her into the main room. "No, I don't, Smoke."

He stooped through the front door into the bright light saying, "Let's go. I want to find me a herd of wild horses."

The branch of the Yellow Cat River that divided his spread from Whelper's forked at the northernmost point and ran west, ending in a pasture of four hundred acres covered with rich native grama grass. Cold water flowed from the boulders and hills behind the pasture to form pools surrounded by willows.

As he let his eye rove the pasture and stream, he whistled. This was great. This was what he had hoped for. He would put his foaling mares up here, he decided.

"What's back of those hills?" he asked as they rested and let the horses suck up the clear sweet water in one of the pools. "No one knows," Smoke Rising said. "But it is part of your land . . . Wash." She had difficulty calling him by his given name.

"That rough back country up there, does it cut into Whelper's spread?"

She studied the sun, then the hills he was referring to. "It must," she finally declared. She looked at him with a slight frown. "We shall turn around now and go straight southwest, into the Yellow Cat Buttes." She pointed. "There is Diamond Peak. And beyond it is Horse Creek River. That is where we will find a manada."

Wash was getting his bearings now. "Yes," he agreed.

"Potter showed me a bit of that barren place." He shook his head in amazement. "I didn't realize wild horses would be on my own land."

"There are two manadas that travel in those buttes. One is led by a black we call Dark Night. He is very old. The other manada is seldom seen. My Cheyenne family came upon them only once in the turning of many suns."

Wash was elated. Everything for his breeding program was here. He only needed money for equipment and tools to fix up the old house. And he needed food and grain for at least two years. His teeth ground together when he thought about his stolen money. Curse those thieves!

Hoshaba broke his thoughts by another of her whinnies!

Wash and Smoke raced together across the pasture, down a narrow coulee and came to a trot only after entering a trail that snaked through the tumbling pile of boulders that would become the Yellow Cat Buttes.

Here, the Horse Creek riverbed was red clay. It twisted at the beginning through walled-in chasms of steep, high bluffs, the sides showing the earthly sedimentation of past eons. Sledge rock of orchid and brown and melon blended into a collage of color and shape that made traveling between its walls an awesome thing. Wash had seen a church once with these same spires and domes.

"Looks like I got myself some wild country. You've been in these buttes before?" Wash was out of breath. Hoshaba was sweating, his ribs bellowing in and out. They had ridden another fifteen miles and the sun was lowering in jagged streamers behind the boulders.

Smoke Rising trotted easily beside him. "To fish," she

said. "And when I surprised the mustangs I returned again." They were on a shelf of rock that dropped into the dry bed of a sluice that curved back into the side of the flat-topped buttes.

She nodded toward one of the draws and led the way.

As they topped the rock-strewn butte they pulled to a stop and Smoke signed to be silent.

Wash stared. Five hundred yards below in a small valley was a manada of twelve to fifteen mustangs. They were grazing, guarded by a black stallion with a mane that touched the ground.

Smoke saw the light in Wash's eye. "This one has some fine mares and he is very old. Maybe someday he can be captured."

Suddenly the sides of Hoshaba filled with air and he whistled a challenge that rolled down the hill and jerked the black's head up. The leader stallion snorted, pawed the ground and answered with a short warning whinny. Nipping his mares into a bunch, he drove them around a boulder and out of sight.

"They are gone," Smoke stated.

"Maybe not," Wash yelled and with a wild "Shooooo!" he charged into the valley. The great horse under him responded with a rush down the steep side of the butte. Here they dodged cactus and thorn bushes, expertly circling the boulder, skidding into the turn that hid the manada.

There! Up that incline, into the timber!

The heaving sides of the red stallion gave him a burst of speed that carried him up the draw into the cedar brake.

Wash's heart beat fast . . . not of fear or strain but with elation. This was what he and Jake had dreamed about.

Yes, he admitted to himself, it was his dream too. "Are you watching, Jake? Are you watching?" he shouted to the wind.

Then Hoshaba's steel jaws clamped tight around the bit and they pulled closer and closer to the frightened mares. The manada slipped and slid over the embankment, backside of the hill. Hoshaba was on their heels. At the bottom, dust swirled in choking clouds, gravel stung their legs as the animals swerved and collided and bunched into a screaming circle.

"Yo!" Wash yelled. He reined hard, at a sharp angle, just in time to miss the cutting hooves of two panicked mares.

Suddenly the black leader stallion whirled and stood aside, defying Hoshaba. Hoshaba ground to a halt and, accepting the challenge, began to paw the dust. "Not now you don't." Then Wash turned cold with fear. The power and instinctive urge of these two stallions would not be easy to quell.

Muttering, "No, boy," through a mouth full of grit, he jerked hard at the smooth bit in Hoshaba's mouth wishing for once he had a sharp-curved one against that stubborn tongue.

Hoshaba's head finally turned away from the stallion, and kicking his heels into the thoroughbred's side, Wash reined him toward a crack in the rocky hillside. The dark coolness of the split must have attracted the hot and sweating Hoshaba. He allowed himself to be driven into it, prancing and switching his plume.

Nerves jangling, Wash trotted Hoshaba to the end of the split that opened into another of the small valleys secreted in these yellow buttes. "That was a narrow miss, you devil," Wash let out in a long breath. Hoshaba nervously side-stepped but Wash was able to keep him from going back.

Wash was unsettled himself and still fearful, but he was excited. If he had been ready with rope and . . . and maybe help he could have. . . .

Smoke Rising shook her head as she pulled alongside. "Wash Buchanan, you are a foolish man."

But her lips wore a tiny smile.

Chapter Twelve

Briley was whistling. He was whistling the only tune he knew, "Sally's moanin', Sally's groanin', Sally's near about to die." Sad words but the tune was nice and Briley felt satisfied and as happy as he ever got.

He had taken his ore to Cheyenne and his money was safe in the First Central Bank. The assay had been good. He supposed he could retire now. But of course he wouldn't. He'd go back to his mine . . . peaceful now, not having to watch his backside, and wait, like Sally, to die.

Asa stopped to munch on a prickly pear apple and Briley reined the grulla to a stop beside her.

He sighed, in such a state of bliss he had to tell her everything. "Them posse-fearing days is over, Asa girl," he said. "If those two wus not after me—and seemin' never heard o' me—then the Whelpers must o' give up. 'Sides, Toliver at the bank says the Whelpers is worried about some new critter in town name of Buchanan."

Briley sniffed, spit to one side of the grulla and snorted a deep belly-laugh. "Toliver near split his britches when I mentioned I might be doin' business with Jack and Lewis Whelper. So what would he advise, I asked. 'Oh, Mr. Briley,' he says, polite-like—I'd said it you see jest to get his reaction to the Whelper boys—he says, 'I wouldn't advise that atall.' "

Briley wiped his mouth and grinned. "Wus then he tol me about them doodlin' with this Buchanan feller. He'd heard about it all the way to Cheyenne, Asa.

"Hee, hee," the old man snickered. "Someone else has riled their backside besides me.

"Wonder whut he done," Briley mumbled.

"Your turn," Wash told Smoke Rising. They were under a grove of cottonwood trees near one of the branches of the Horse Creek river. He had finally gotten his wind and nerves back after his run with the mustangs. But he was tired and the sun was low in the west.

Smoke Rising took Hoshaba's reins, grinned as Wash hefted her into the saddle that towered a foot above her head, and clicked the stallion into a gallop. "Not too far, we need to start for home." Wash smiled then settled into a weary rest under one of the cottonwoods.

He nodded once, then opened his eyes to glance at the nearby hilltop. Instantly he was awake. His eye had caught the sharp, brilliant glitter of sunlight.

He sat up and studied the rocks and grooves along the ridge of the hill. Nothing could produce such a blinding flash of light unless it was man-made. And it was usually sun glancing off a mirror, or knife, or rifle barrel.

Wash ran his hand through his hair and eased himself to a standing position, ignoring the hill.

Smoke and Hoshaba came trotting into the cottonwood grove and he could tell by the way she rode she too had seen the flashes of light.

Smoke slid off Hoshaba and with her opposite hand grabbed Sister's halter. "We must leave," she said quietly.

"I know. And Smoke, I want you to do something for me. I want you to start out with me . . . and when we reach that line of rocks straight along the ravine that leads back to town . . . I want you to kick that little mare for all she's worth and make for home."

Smoke Rising was about to say something but Wash broke in.

"Do it, Smoke! And don't look back. Hoshaba and I will be going another way. You hear?"

"Yes," she answered, "But. . . ."

"Please."

Five minutes later Wash gently broke away from Smoke Rising, reined into a sandy slough and whipped the tired stallion into a run. "Sorry old boy," he mumbled. "Looks like Whelper and his dogs didn't take my advice. Let's go!"

A short rang out. Darn, they were good. Already on his heels. They'd not be waiting for a confab this time.

Another shot zizzed over their heads and Wash felt the stallion's withers tremble, the horse shy toward the right. He's never been shot at but he knows when to be afraid, Wash thought.

When another slug kicked up the sand at Hoshaba's front hooves the stallion took the bit between his teeth and burst into that ground-eating lunge he had used the day in St. Louis when Wash first tested him.

Wash's heart ached. You're already tired. You're too tired, he thought. We'll never outrun those thieves.

When a rock wall rose steeply near their right, Wash decided to chance a dodge. At the end of the wall he swerved into the opening and reined down a steep incline. To his gut-wrenching horror he realized too late it was no out. The gully was opening onto the prairie encircled by that cursed gorge. "Oh, no," Wash muttered, swallowing bitter spit. "We're trapped."

Two riders careened from the ravine behind them. Three others appeared in front, two hundred yards to their right. Wash pulled Hoshaba to miss them but another horseman with raised rifle bounded in from the west flank.

Wash hunched lower in the saddle. Another bullet popped beside him. This one left a red stain on his arm.

They'll kill us both, Shaba, he thought.

Zing. Another bullet tore a groove along Hoshaba's neck. Wash cursed. "But not without a run!" he roared.

The gorge. Where was that drop-off into eternity called Wild Horse Gorge?

Briley climbed a hill across the Horse Creek river. He was around the gorge now, safe on the far side of old Francis Ross's spread. But it was still a wearisome three miles to his cabin. He stopped under some willows to rest. "Maybe I'll camp here for the night," he told Asa just as the echoing sound of rifle fire pulled his tired old shoulders into a tight pinch.

"Goldurn! Wus I wrong about them Whelpers? They still after me?" He humped over to his pack and jerked up the Winchester. Squinting his eyes to see across the gorge he picked up riders coming from several directions. They fired as they rode in and bunched together behind a big red horse carrying a man not daring to look back.

His eyes blood-red and stinging, Wash sought the break in the earth that meant a sudden fall onto sharp boulders. When the ground changed color and texture on his left he realized that was the beginning of the great earth split.

He guided Hoshaba steadily, keeping the edge of the chasm three hundred yards away. He would need speed to jump.

"It's our only chance," he told Hoshaba. "You can do it. You've jumped higher and longer." But Wash Buchanan did not believe it. A knot twisted inside and exploded into a sob as he sighed the grove of trees near the edge of the chasm. Where Potter said maybe . . . maybe a horse could jump.

Hoshaba stumbled, his front knees skidding into the gravel. Wash tumbled across his neck, wetting his face in the bloody wound. Instantly he gathered the reins tighter, yanking upward to raise Hoshaba's head.

Horse and rider lurched up and without breaking stride drew near the trees.

Briley mounted the grulla and booted him into a rocky ravine. As soon as they came out of it Briley reined to a halt, climbed behind one of the highest rocks and stood amazed at the spectacle.

He was close now. He could see the men clearly as they raced in a line over the prairie. He knew four of them. Stoop Nettles rode the pinto, the bald-headed guy everyone called Slick rode a grey, and Lewis and

Jack . . . goosebumps coarsed up Briley's neck! Those butchers were running down some poor fellow, shooting to kill.

"That's Buchanan, I reckon," Briley muttered and climbed off the rock. He mounted and started the grulla, holding the Winchester in his right hand. He'd get at least one shot.

On the curve before the grove of trees on the other side, Briley watched the big red horse stumble, gather himself up and strike out for the gorge itself. "Whut?. . . ." Briley could not believe what he was watching. The man was going to jump Wild Horse Gorge!

". . . fffew . . . more . . . yards . . . see it? See it!" Wash cried.

Hoshaba eyed the split, snorted.

"Ready, boy, ready," Wash pleaded with voice and body.

Twenty yards further he wheeled Hoshaba to the left to face the chasm. His knees clinging tight enough to draw blood, Wash whispered, "ready, ready, . . . NOW!"

Hosahba gathered his great haunches and propelled himself out . . . and over Wild Horse Gorge.

Wash heard a barrage of bullets. Felt the ground depart from under them. And then a jolt like he'd never had in his life. His head cracked back on his neck, his arms flew up, his body was slung over the saddle. But the sound that tore Wash Buchanan's heart was the sharp crack, like breaking tinder, as Hoshaba's legs hit the ground on the opposite side of the chasm.

Chapter Thirteen

Smoke Rising slid off Sister in front of the sheriff's office. Stumbling inside she stammered, "Sheriff Miles . . . please, you must ride out to the Ross place . . . near the buttes . . . I'll show you. Come."

Elias Miles was nailing a wanted poster on the wall. He stopped wheezing when he saw her. Darn, she got better looking every day. "Hold on," he said. "What are you talking about?"

"Some men with rifles are in the breaks near the river and Wash Buchanan is there. We ran but I'm afraid they. . . ."

"You sayin' some men are trailing Buchanan?"

"Yes. And with all his trouble I'm certain they will kill him."

Miles laughed. "You see these men?"

"Yes. Please, get some help."

"Were they trailing Buchanan?"

Smoke nervously rubbed her sweaty arms. He was not

going to do anything. Why had she ever hoped he would? "I did not see them, I was going for help. But I know they were after him."

"Well then, I guess we can go take a looksee if you want. You and me." He picked his hat off the hook and hitched his pants up.

Smoke Rising was out the door. "Never mind," she mumbled.

Ed was watering the horses in the stable. He agreed with her there might be trouble but what could they do? They'd get themselves killed too if they rode out there. Besides, Buchanan and that stallion could outrun any horse around.

Smoke Rising sat on a bale of hay and tried to think. Wash had done the right thing by ordering her away. He had freedom to outmaneuver the riders if they really were Whelper's men. But maybe they were simply hunting and they both had come to a wrong conclusion. Her Cheyenne senses told her otherwise.

"I'm frightened, Lowery," she said quietly.

He put a stubby hand on her shoulder. "Tomorri, if he ain't come back we'll go out. Now you get some rest, all the chores is done til mornin'."

Smoke Rising could not rest. She went to the Trail End and asked at the desk if Mr. Washington Buchanan had returned to his room. The sleepy-eyed clerk grumped a, "No, miss." And went back to snoring.

Realizing she could do no more, she lay on her cot behind the livery and finally fell into a restless sleep.

She was up before daybreak. She put on her moccasins, tied a blanket into a roll along with clean white rags—he might be wounded—and leaping onto Sister's bone-hard, rangy back she headed toward the buttes on the Ross land.

Dew sparkled on the stiff grass when she stooped to study the prints she and Wash had made as they split from one another in the gully. Hers took off to the south without interference. The big prints of Hoshaba were clear until he reached the rock barrier on the west, then she saw where the riders came out of the buttes and overtook them.

With a stillness in her throat, Smoke Rising followed the tracks to the softer sand of the slough, then up the embankment to the timber and around that to the open prairie before Wild Horse Gorge.

"Oh Great Wise One Above," she wailed. "They drove him into the trap."

Her eyes scouted ahead on the ground, over the edge of the field, all the way to the great chasm on the left.

At the grove of stunted cedar trees she dropped to her knees and with a catch in her chest looked across the gulf. A sob choked her when she saw the hump . . . the still, red-brown hump that was surely the body of Hoshaba.

Smoke Rising leapt astride Sister and raced back and around the lower edge of the yellow buttes. It took her two hours and by the time she reached the body of the fallen horse she was weak and trembling.

She kneeled beside the dead stallion. His great eye was staring and hard. When she touched one flag-furled ear she saw the round bullet hole in his forehead where his spirit had drained out. How did that happen? she wondered. That he could be shot in the forehead. Another tear in his neck came from a bullet from the rear—as it should. Then she noticed the front legs, twisted, swollen, broken. Had Wash shot the stallion? Where was Wash?

Frantic, Smoke Rising whirled to call his name. "Wash Buchanan!" she called loudly. Perhaps he was hiding. Perhaps he was wounded. She studied the ground, the low bushes nearby, a clump of cholla cactus in a low place. Then . . . "There. Oh Great Father," she silently cried, "there is a grave."

Fresh red clay was heaped three feet wide and six feet long in a rugged pile. A belt had been placed across it. Smoke picked up the belt and recognized Wash's belt-buckle. She could not read the letters but she knew his belt.

"Who found you?" she whispered. "Who came upon you so soon and found you to give you a burial?"

Not the Whelpers. Their tracks had not followed to this side. Hastily she looked again. Now she saw them. The faint tracks of a small donkey or burro and those of one man whose boots were worn and lop-sided.

Her head full of pain and questions, Smoke Rising fell in a quivering heap beside the earth pile and laying her head across it began to chant the song of spirit death.

She chanted until the heat of the sun drove her to water. She drank long and deep and then began to gather stones. One by one she piled them against the great horse who would never again race with joy over the fields of grama grass. Each rock was a curse upon Whelper and his kin and she resolved with the deliberate placing of each sun-blistered stone to find a way to kill the man.

She hummed in a strong monotone as she worked and when the stones were all around the horse, she began to pile them upon his body. Then she stood between the grave and the stones and sang a Cheyenne prayer. The words calmed her, made her feel as if she were with her people again, not suffering alone.

The Whelpers must believe it is I who buried them, she decided. With a cedar switch she carefully wiped away the prints of the man and donkey.

When late shadows of the trees and boulders grew long, bending into the chasm itself, Smoke Rising climbed on Sister and began to travel slowly back to town, unfeeling except for the fist of anger in her heart.

Chapter Fourteen

The smell of coffee, fresh and strong and full of memory pulled Wash Buchanan back into the world. He lifted one shoulder off the rough canvas but the pain was too strong.

Later, he roused again. Then cried out and sank back into the safety of sleep.

Haunting images of a giant golden-red horse seared his eyelids, the massive chest of the stallion pulsed and heaved, its thin legs coiled like springs to lift it higher and higher to miss the bullets, to jump the great gorge.

Wash cried out as horse and man hit the ground.

Heat. Waves of it smothered him, cut off his breath, sent him deeper and deeper into the hole of sleep.

Now the hole was cold. He shivered violently. He shook and throbbed and sweat blood. A piece of hot coal lay on his rib, burning through to the other side. Another piece pressed into his chin.

Floods of sickness gripped his stomach. He fought

against the heavy clamps that pinned him to the ground but his strength was gone. He was weak, dog-tired, and he wanted only to forget. To forget and to go away. . . .

Later, he opened his eyes to see a man sitting on a stump. The man said, "Name's Briley. And you're old man Ross's grandson, Wash Buchanan, come from St. Louis. Found thet out in Cheyenne and later in Granite when I dropped in to see 'bout a matter."

The man was old and yet not old. His beard shagged over a lean stomach but the beard was grey and his face was criss-crossed with wrinkles. He wore an ancient raw-leather vest.

Wash closed his eyes. His side throbbed. He was thirsty.

"Need a drink?" The man Briley nodded toward a low-burning fire beside the pallet where Wash lay. A coffee pot bubbled and sang to him, but he could not move.

After a while Briley said "Pshaw," and leaning over poured the scalding black brew into a tin cup. He set the cup on the ground beside Wash's right hand.

"There tis," he said. "Have yourself a drink."

The smell was torture but Wash could not move. Dared not move. The pain would kill him.

"It's up to you, boy. But you been lying here long enough. If you don't stir them muscles pretty soon, they'll clamp down forever." Briley began coiling and uncoiling a long rope.

Wash turned his face away. "Let me die," he muttered.

"Huh," Briley snorted. "Not after all I done. And not when we need each other, boy. You and me are going to work together. Yes sir, I've done decided it's time to turn the tables on them lyin' Whelpers. And I 'magine you want it too. They done this, you recall."

Wash looked around at the old man. His tongue was dry and thick. It hurt to breathe but he said, "Did . . . did you find him?"

"That red horse?" Briley laid down the rope and plucking a small rock from a pile at his feet, began hacking at it with a hammer. "Yep. Matter o' fact I saw it happen. You can be proud o' that stallion, son. He fair leaped across that crack in the earth and paid for it with two broke legs." After a few seconds Briley glanced over at him and added, "O'course I eased him out of his hurtin' with a bullet right quick-like."

Wash winced with pain as great gulping sobs spilled from his chest. Each sob tore through his body like a thousand knives but he could not stop.

Later, when his crying had drained the last drop of moisture from his body, Wash tightened his muscles and heaved himself into a sitting position. He stayed that way, panting, waiting for his sight to clear. Where was Briley?

Wash clutched the cup of coffee that was now cool and with a tremor that shook half of it out, gulped it down in one swig.

More. He needed more. Where was that old man? Why couldn't he give him some water? Wash lay back down, cursing the man Briley for leaving him alone.

The sun was now in his face. He glanced around. Where was this place? He did not recognize it. It was a small clearing surrounded by high rock walls of yellow sandy sledge, like the buttes west of his land. A grove of cottonwood trees stood one hundred yards away. Why hadn't the old man put him under that? Blast him, it was broiling hot in the sun.

Wash began to crawl toward the trees. Anger at old Briley drove him grumbling toward its shade. He collapsed there and went to sleep.

When he woke the sun was setting. His thirst was agony. "Briley . . . get me some water!"

Wash sat up, glanced in a circle. To his astonishment he saw a cabin. It was against the towering wall of a hill two hundred yards away. This was crazy. Where was he? Why hadn't the old codger put him in the cabin?

Standing was unbearable but Wash stood. Now he could hear water running. Near the far side of the trees was a green spot. A small fawn-colored horse was cropping grass. And the water he heard was a stream.

Wash stumbled, fell, got up, walked, fell, then finally crawled until his face was submerged in the free-running creek and he was gulping the cold, sweet water.

He sat awhile watching the gelding. He wondered about the cabin, it couldn't be too far away from the gorge.

At the thought of Wild Horse Gorge and Hoshaba, a knot of anger and pain bore down on him. He sat rocking back and forth, wishing he had died with his horse.

He must have fallen asleep again. The next thing he knew it was night. He sat up, rubbed his hand through his stiff hair. Full of dried blood, he guessed.

There was a light in the cabin. Wash took another long drink from the stream then started toward the light.

A wild "Heeee—Hawwww!" sent his heart pounding just as he came to the cabin step. A short, lop-earned burro was eating something out of a pan. Wash pushed past it and stumbled into the light.

"Good," the man Briley stated when he saw Wash. "I tol' Asa you'd either git up or die. Figured it best to let you decide for yourself. Sit." He pointed to a cane-bottomed chair near the table and Wash fell into it.

"Supper is near ready. You like poached rabbit?"

Wash held his head in his hand with his elbow resting on the table. "Not hungry."

"You didn't pick ore all day, did ye?" Briley lovingly set a platter in the middle of the table and stepped back to admire his fixings.

The smell opened Wash's eyes. His hand dropped. The large shallow bowl was heaped full of rabbit, each piece browned and dripping with juice. Crusty-skinned potatoes swam in a thick gravy around the meat. Some sort of white root vegetable was piled to one side. Briley plopped a basket of sourdough biscuits onto the table and sat down to help himself.

Wash's stomach growled. He accepted a cup of coffee then decided to try a potato.

Thirty minutes later they both pushed back and sighed. "That was good," Wash managed. Maybe the old man was not so bad after all.

"Don't reckon you got any broke bones, seeing' you walked up here." Briley wiped his mouth with a dirty rag. "Now we can git down to business. Everone thinks you're dead you see. I sorta buried you."

Wash frowned. "You buried me?"

"Yea. So's they'd not come lookin' fer you any more. So's we'll be free to do what orta be done. Now, in a few more days you'll be fittin' enough to begin."

Wash stared. "Begin what?"

Briley stepped over to a shelf, took down a handgun and placed it on the table. It looked new. It was huge, its barrel the longest Wash had ever seen. When Briley turned it around the black handle was right in front of him.

"Bought it new yestiday. Went in to Granite—huh," Briley chortled, thinking of the days past when he had been afraid to set his foot in town. "Bought this beauty from off the keeper of that gun and saddle shop. Don't need no saddle, I brung in the one you wus usin'. Anyway, look at this here shooter."

With his hands on the edge of the table, Wash shoved himself away from the gun.

Briley nodded at it and said, "Paid double for it o' course, but it's a spankin' new Colt single action, the kind the army uses. It's a .45 caliber, five and a half inch barrel. She'll hit a might to the left 'cause o' the rifling, but we'll watch for thet."

Wash stood up and went over to the iron stove, poured himself a fresh cup of coffee and began to sip, not looking at Briley.

Briley was not deterred. "Whilst I was there I had Finney cut the trigger off and hone it down real good. Without no trigger one movement'll do it all. There'll never be a better pistol, Buchanan."

"What's this all about, Briley?" Wash asked, the shadow of what was coming already setting his teeth on edge.

"It's about you and me going after them men whut killed your horse and near killed you. It's about when you learn to fire this .45 good enough to hit a man . . . then we'll go after them Whelpers. That's what it's about."

Wash Buchanan locked his gaze onto the gun. A weapon one man could use to settle the arguments of a dozen men. The law of this country. Maybe what the old man said was true. Maybe it was time to stop Jack Whelper himself.

He hefted the pistol, feeling its balance. Despite his reluctance he found himself saying, "You may be right, Briley, but I can't go out and shoot a man in cold blood . . . not even Jack Whelper. I have no real evidence he shot my grandfather.

"But the man is a viper and he needs stopping."

Briley said, "Humph! Whut you propose then?"

"We'll be the law ourselves, do what it should do. We'll get evidence, then round the culprits up and bring them in."

"They'll just be let go, boy."

"No. We'll turn them over to a U.S. Marshall. I've notified one already, though I'm worried. There's been time for him to get here."

"If'n you sent the telegram yourself it never went. Whelper'll have his hand on that too."

"We'll see. In the meantime I'll take your gun."

Chapter Fifteen

"I need some answers, Briley," Wash stated the next morning. He and Briley were under the cottonwoods near the creek. Briley had cleaned and oiled the new pistol, explaining its workings as he went. Now he was rubbing an oil rag over his old Dragoon. Wash had the Colt in his hands, turning it, pulling back the hammer, aiming it at trees, getting the feel of a gun.

"Whut you need to know?"

"Where are we? Who are you and why do you want to go after the Whelpers?"

Briley drew a breath. It had been a long time since he had spoken out loud—to another human being—about Mary Rose and little Mary Argent. Briley cleared his throat and said, "In sixty I was workin' for Russ Whelper. That was Jack and Lewis's old man. Besides his cattle he owned a store in town. I was on in years even then, but I found Mary Rose and she and me got married and had a little'n, a girl we called Little Mary. She was a darlin', 'bout five years old." Briley sniffed and wiped his nose with his fingers.

"I'd found this here mountain and the silver in it and Mary Rose and me wus waitin' til we could buy it before we moved on out here. We'd come here to have a picnic and spend the day dreaming over living here. Those were good days, Buchanan, when we wus all together, me, Mary Rose, and Mary 'Argent'."

Wash frowned at the unusual name and Briley said, "Yea, it sounds 'culiar, but you see, we began callin' Little Mary after the treasure we'd found. Mary Rose was French and she said the word for silver was 'argent'." Briley uttered the word softly, then cut off a plug of tobacco.

After a moment he continued. "Then Ruff Whelper taken a shine to Mary Rose. Kept after her in mean low-down ways. She was frightened but she wanted me to hold on and not lay into him like I wanted. Like I should've. I never dreamed he'd be the snake he wus.

"Heck, he set me up. Sent a note for me to come back to the store late one night, saying for me to check some papers in his safe . . . give me the number o' the safe. Darn! whut a fool I wus. Just as I got to the store I heard a shot from inside. A feller come running out shoutin' 'Oh, it wus Whelper, it wus Whelper!' "

"I taken off, but it wus too late to clear my name. Whelper told the sheriff with his dyin' breath that it wus me what shot him, tryin' to steal from his safe."

Wash broke in. "Then you must be Jess Kendall . . . Simmons said a Jess Kendall shot Whelper."

"Yea, that's my real tab but I had to call myself different you know. And jus keep on acallin' me Briley."

"Are you saying this fellow that you saw running out was a hired gun meant to shoot *you?*"

"Yep. That's it. But everone believed Ruff Whelper. And after he died they come after me, posse and wanted-money and all. Ruff left the two boys with a brother named Lofton and those three hounded me for years."

Wash let the gun rest in his hand. Watching Briley relive his loss was unsettling. He thought Briley needed asking in order for him to finish his tale and so he said very quietly, "What happened to Mary Rose and the girl? Simmons told me people thought they died, that true?"

"I guess. I left them with a friend widder lady that lived out a good ways, not far from a camp o' Indans. She told me when I come back for 'em that Mary Rose took Little Mary and up and left. Said they were both real sick and she begged 'em not to go . . . but. . . ."

"I'm sorry Briley. And all these years you've thought the Whelpers were still hunting you?"

"Were, til now. When you come along they began on you. Why is that, boy? Why they after you?"

Gripping the handle of the gun in a tight fist, Wash shook his head sharply. "I had a run in with Jack about Hoshaba—that's the name of the stallion." Wash added this with a quick glance toward the heavens. Then he said, "And he didn't like it when I talked to the girl who works at the livery. He had me beat up and my money stolen."

Wash stood up, shoving bullets into the cylinder as he'd seen Briley do. "I think he probably killed my grandfather. I don't know why, except he wants to own the ranch my grandfather left me."

Briley set an empty tin can on a rock under one of the cottonwoods. "Your granpa had a good place, but heck,

Whelper don't need more land. He owns clear to the Platte. Maybe that's one o' the things we can find out when we get that buzzard under our sights."

"Yea. Well, okay. Now I know who you are and why you want to get Whelper. But where are we?" Wash glanced around the buttes and hills surrounding them.

"Three misery-miles from the gorge. That mustang o' mine near broke down atotin' you. Asa carried yore saddle and I walked. This here is a place to hide. No one ever comes. Too twisted and rocky and nothing here when you get here." He snorted. "Cept that silver mine, and it's hidden better'n a chaw in a fat man's jaw." Briley grinned and spat.

"You really get silver from this mountain?"

"Enough so's I have to make two, three trips a year to have it changed into bank money. You see, I've worked this ore hill these sixteen year. I'm rich, boy." Briley pinched his nose between his eyes and added, "The only thing I hanker for is to tell Whelper I'm no thief and that his pa was a rotten skunk. And then shoot 'im."

The old man handed Wash a worn leather holster. "Put this on and stick that shooter in it. It's better than a new one, it's soft, rubbed smooth, and I put new taler inside. Now you pull that .45 in and out til you can do it without it hanging up."

Wash slipped the holster around his waist and tied the piggin string around his leg. It felt comfortable, as if it had been *his* for sixteen years. He worked the six-gun into it, pulled it out and aimed. Again and again. Finally he turned to Briley and said, "Can you do something for me, Briley?"

"Huh. Haven't I already?"

Wash smiled. "Yea, I guess so. And thanks. But I need to let someone know I'm alive. I know you say we should hole up til we're ready and I agree. But a girl was riding with me at the gorge and I want her to know I'm alive. You say no one recognizes you in town, then it should be safe for you to see her."

"Tell me where to find her," Briley said and taking the pistol from Wash, thumbed back the hammer and blasted the empty can atop the rock under the cottonwood. "Now you do it," he said.

Wash tried to thumb the hammer. His thumb slipped and he dropped the gun in the dirt.

Briley shook his head. "Take some practice. Here, use this part o' yore thumb, not the end. Where you say this gal is?"

"She's the one that got Whelper riled up when I spoke to her. She works at Ed Lowery's Livery. Calls herself Smoke Rising." Wash hefted the seven pound pistol, aimed, thumbed the hammer back, and blasted the tree limbs over the tin can sitting on the rock.

"That's a Indan name. She Indan?" Briley grabbed the pistol, aimed at the can and knocked it off the rock.

"No, but some Cheyenne raised her. She's a friend, Briley. And Briley, while you're in town get me a mount. I'll pay you when I get my money back." Wash held the gun again, took aim and shot bark off the cottonwood.

Briley grunted and took back the pistol. "Can't buy no horse in town, son. They'll wonder since I got me one already. Nope. We'll git you a horse, don't worry. Now watch this."

Chapter Sixteen

Smoke Rising brushed the tail of a white mare who had been ridden through a thicket of burrs. She moved around the flank with one hand touching the mare's rump.

"Too bad your lovin' way with four-footed critters don't stretch to two-legged ones . . . your fellow man so to speak." Jack Whelper sauntered in, looked around and leaned himself against the stall post. He picked his teeth with a straw and looked her up and down with a steel-hard squint. He had a handsome face, his features even and strong. His eyes gave him away.

Smoke Rising jumped at the sound of his voice. She thought she was alone. Where was Lowery, she wondered?

"Come sit with me at the Drovers, I'll fix us up a back room where we'll not be bothered. You need a good stiff drink. You never leave this stinkin' place."

"Leave me alone, Jack Whelper," her voice was deep and slow.

"Untouchable, huh?" Whelper threw his straw drown and wiping his mouth with the back of his hand, he stepped closer. "Still pining over that city man?" Now he was serious and angry. He grabbed her long single plait and with a yank whirled her around and pulled her to his chest.

She pushed and wiggled, deploring his hot whiskey breath. He tightened his grip and bent to her ear whispering, "I told you he won't be coming back, girl. He's left for good. Now you think about me." Pinning her arms to her sides, he pressed his mouth to her neck and over her flushed face.

"No! Leave me alone," she demanded through gritted teeth. Turning her head violently from side to side to escape his wet kisses she raised her right knee and slammed it up into him.

"Darn you wildcat!" he cried and dropped his hands. He lowered his head, his eyes closed. When his head came up he wore a twisted sneer on his lips. "I'll give you what you want then," he growled and backhanded her into the wall.

The white horse whinnied and side-stepped, her hooves just missing Smoke Rising's moccasined feet. The girl slid down the wall with a groan. Whelper grinned and stooped to pull her to him again. This time he slapped her cheek then pushed her further back into the stall, under the mare's stomping hooves.

Smoke Rising felt the swish and sting of the hooves as they danced by her legs, scraping her left thigh, She shoved herself backward, across the hay-strewn floor with her hands under her seat. Heat roared in her veins. Whelper would pay for this.

Then she remembered Wash Buchanan.

"Wait," she cried, one hand out as if in surrender. "I . . . I know he's dead."

At the change in her voice Whelper stood still. "So, you're ready to admit he's gone."

"Yes. As a matter of fact it was me who . . . who buried him." Smoke Rising was now standing, slowly walking out of the stall, one hand rubbing her bruised thigh. She passed Whelper and reaching into a ruck sack pulled out the belt.

Whelper stared at the buckle. "I found him across the gorge beside the stallion. He fell . . . evidently trying to jump." Smoke handed the belt to Whelper and he took it, studying the letters on the buckle: W.M.B.

"You ordered him killed," she said flatly, her cheek burning like a coal of fire. "Why, Jack Whelper? Why did you hate him?"

Jack tossed the belt onto the ruck sack. "You didn't see me there, did you?"

She snorted. "No, you hire your dirty work done." With a hard shove she pushed Whelper against the mare. At the same time she reached under the horse's belly and gave her a mean pinch.

The rear hooves catapulted up and back, knocking the already flailing man crashing into the boards. The mare stomped, backing over Whelper, one hoof crunching his knee. The stricken man folded into a ball.

Some deep, hidden core within her overrode her desire to kill. Smoke Rising pulled the frightened mare forward, speaking in her slow throaty Cheyenne tongue.

Whelper gagged, swaying into the straw. He lay still, moaning.

"Next time I'll let her finish the job," Smoke Rising promised. "You weren't worthy to lick Wash Buchanan's boots."

She stood with clenched fists, her anger near tears. She stiffened her shoulders and warned, "Keep on the watch, Jack Whelper. Never turn your back, never close an eye without someone to guard you. I'm Cheyenne-raised, remember? And the Cheyenne are a sneakin', killin' breed."

She hurried out of the livery with her head down. She needed a drink and a place to cool off.

"Miss . . . uh . . . Smoke Rising?" Elizabeth Drennan was about to pass when she stopped and called. "I've been wanting to see you. Could we talk?" She gave a little squeak when whe saw the slap mark on Smoke Rising's cheek and her rumpled, straw-covered clothes.

"Are you hurt, my dear?" she asked.

Smoke Rising shook her head, said nothing.

Elizabeth touched the girl's elbow, leading her toward a buggy. "Let's go to my house and have a drink."

Smoke Rising had no resistance. She let herself be led. The buggy stopped at the front porch of the large white-pillared house on the opposite end of town. They sat on white cane chairs on the shaded porch.

A maid brought a pitcher of sweet lemon water—with ice. Smoke Rising had never had ice in the summer and wondered where it came from. It sent a rivilet of coolness down her parched throat. So, she thought, this is how Elizabeth Drennan lives.

"I believe you and Wash are . . . were . . . friends," Elizabeth began. "I've been hearing terrible things. That he has gone back to St. Louis. Or that he is . . . well, dead. Smoke Rising, do you know what's happened to Wash Buchanan?"

Smoke Rising looked at Elizabeth's long white hands. She wore a gold ring with a stone that was as green as her eyes. Then she looked at the girl's worried half-smile. She loves Wash, Smoke Rising decided. She should know.

"This is a mean town, Miss Drennan. It allowed Wash Buchanan to be beaten, his money to be stolen, and his great horse to be killed."

Elizabeth gasped and leaned on the table as if she would faint.

"Wash himself was killed with Hoshaba. I found them, buried Hoshaba. But someone else had been there before me and buried Wash."

"Who?"

"I do not know who dug the grave for Wash but I know who killed him. Jack Whelper killed him."

"Are you sure? Why doesn't Sheriff Miles know . . . he seems to think Wash went back to St. Louis."

"This is a one man town, Miss Drennan. And the vulture Jack Whelper is that man."

Elizabeth's eyes filled with tears. She reached out and touched Smoke Rising's hand. "Thank you for telling me. If I can ever help you in any way, let me know."

Smoke Rising rose to go. There was no more to say. And what help could Elizabeth Drennan ever give?

Chapter Seventeen

"Now listen careful, Buchanan. We don't have time fer you to learn to shoot ever which aways. So I'll give you the quickest, the one thet comes by instinct if its done right. See thet rock, see thet hump, see thet tree? Well, they make a twenty foot circle, the distance fer shootin' fastest and surest. And you'll pull and shoot like this."

Briley suddenly jerked his hand forward and up, scooping the .45 out of the holster, thumbing back the hammer and firing as the pistol left the pocket.

Wash Buchanan laughed. He couldn't help it. The movement was so unlike the old codger. It was fast and beautiful. "You didn't even take time to hold and aim, did you?"

"Nope. Thet's the trick. You 'point' this here gun at whatever you want to hit like you would point your finger at a feller—except since it pulls aways to the left 'cause of the rifling in the barrel you always point a mite to the right."

Wash took the gun and holster. "You're supposing our targets will be within a twenty foot range, are you?"

"We'll try fer it, boy. Else it'll be rifles at a distance and thet won't git me no satisfaction. I want to see Jack and Lewis squirm."

"Fair enough. And I want to take them in if we can. Now what about my horse? We going to catch a mustang?"

Briley humphed, "You think thet's crazy but you'll see. Lookit the grulla. Caught him 'bout five years after I holed up here. He's done me fine."

Wash was silent at that and curious. "There's a manada led by a black in the buttes west of *my* place. They what you're thinking of?"

"Nope. Thet stallion is old, he'll never be rode. There's a smaller bunch thet's led by a dun. He'll be whut we're after. He's young and tough as dry leather. When you get him you'll never want another." Briley paused then added. "If you can break 'im. You any good at horse breakin'?"

"I'll give it a try," Wash said with his blood running hot. How many times had he taken an untamed bronc and gentled him into a saddle horse? He loved the challenge.

"What's this dun look like?"

"Right small. Not sixteen hands like thet red o' yours. More like fourteen. He's got a black tail and mane, with a black stripe down his back where a polecat has white."

Wash nodded. "A line-back dun they're called. The

stripe and markings show he has no inbreeding with later Spanish horses. He's of pure wild stock."

When Briley coughed Wash explained, "I made it my business to find out as much as I could about these wild horses. You see, I planned to breed the red stallion with mustang mares. That's why I came to Wyoming, Briley."

Wash waited for the lump in his throat to dissolve then asked, "Where do we find this manada?"

"I know where the dun waters his mares ever two days. He makes a circle with his grazing and he hits a right smart big pool thet's north o' here. Thet's where we'll git him."

Briley whispered, "The wind's in our favor, carrying our scent south so when he comes he'll not pick up neither you nor me. He'll be driving his mares down that incline to git to the pool."

Briley and Wash were lying on their stomachs overlooking a small valley backed by one of those tumbling, hill-high boulders that were strewn along creeks and branches of the Yellow Cat River in these northern buttes. This creek ended in a pool that cupped itself into the side of a boulder with a single outlet on the far side. That was the escape route if the mustangs were confronted from the valley side.

"Now remember whut I told you. You circle on foot 'round to thet back side and set yourself near thet crack. If you keep back til they're in the water he'll not spook. Now, when the mares are a'drinking, I'll come in and drive them through the pool and out the crack. Then the stallion goes into the water—thinking he'll git out the far side like his troop. When I whistle you step out and rope him whilst he's in the water."

Wash squirmed. "I don't like this, Briley. In the water?"

"Only way to git this critter. He's little but he's smart and tricky. You'd not git a rope on him on dry land. He'd break your neck and his too."

Wash sighed, shook his head to clear his thoughts. He wasn't sure he could pull this off. "Okay, then what?"

"Then I'll throw another rope on 'im and we'll let him swim til he's nigh wore down. When I whistle agin you jump in, git astraddle, and ride 'im out."

"Without a harness or bridle." Wash was stupified.

"You can twist a halter out o' the rope on his neck if you wont, 'fore you git on him."

"This sounds unbelievable, Briley. Have you ever done this? Is this the way you caught the grulla?"

"Nope. Caught him accidental like when he fell in deep sand. But this here is the way Indans do it. Now, Buchanan," Briley was about to add something else Wash didn't want to hear. He looked away.

Briley cleared his throat and spat a stream of tobacco to one side. "You see, Buchanan, once you git on the dun . . . why, he's yours. Whatever you do to break him is up to you. So, for a while you'll not need me. I've got beans and bread here, and there's cartridges aplenty for your shootin'. I figure it'll take you some days.

"If'n . . . huh, when . . . *when* you git the dun broke you ride on back to the cabin. Meantimes, I'll go into town and tell thet girl you're alive."

Wash was speechless. He picked up his hat and rope and started his climb toward the farside of the valley.

Briley muttered suddenly, too late for Wash to hear, "You can swim, can't ye?"

Chapter Eighteen

It was late afternoon. The August day had been stifling but already it was cooler. Night in this high country would be cold.

Behind the huge granite boulder Wash placed himself in a niche. If he leaned around, he could see the pool. He was doubtful this idea of Briley's would work. He would go along if it didn't get too dangerous, but he'd not kill himself trying to catch a wild stallion that would be too little to ride if he caught it. He was six feet two and weighed one hundred and eighty pounds. No fourteen hand horse could carry him for long.

Smoke Rising . . . what would she think of this trick? He leaned out and studied the valley. No sign yet of the manada.

Then he heard them. A whinny, a whistle, tramping of hooves. He pulled back out of sight against the stone wall.

Now came the sound of water splashing, mud squishing, a stallion further away sounding his cry, coming closer. Wash dared a glance around the boulder and saw in amazement the pool aswarm with mares and colts. Suddenly lunging out of the pool on his side, so close they touched his sleeve, they came pounding up the slope and crowding through the split. Wash's heart beat so fast he could feel it in his neck. How would he ever. . . .

"Wheeeeeee!" came Briley's whistle. Wash slapped the rump of the last mare as she whipped around the crack and out into the open. Then he stepped through the nick to see the dun swimming toward him.

"Throw your rope," yelled Briley.

Wash swung his rope overhead, sighted the dun as it thrashed in the water, and sailed the coil into the air to drop over the stallion's head. Wash smiled. He never missed a lasso.

The stallion bobbed up and down in the pool, fighting now to reach the other shore. Then Briley's rope settled over him and reach the other shore. Then Briley's rope settled over him and tightened around his neck. "We got 'im!" shouted Briley. "Now let's work 'im good, make him swim! Make 'im swim!"

The two men worked in unison, pulling or loosening as the frantic animal churned the pool to a muddy froth.

Wash's arms were tired, once he thought he'd have to let go. But Briley kept up a barrage of shouts and whistles that would not let either him or the dun give up.

The horse floundered, his head went under. Wash yanked on his rope, hoping to bring him to the surface. When he thought the animal would drown, his nose popped up and those dark, wild eyes sought the shore again.

"Jump in!" Briley commanded, flailing his rope to hit the stallion's ears, urging the mustang around once more.

Wash bit his bottom lip, dropped his end of the rope. Blast the man, this was the craziest stunt he'd ever seen.

"Go!" Briley yelled again.

Wash jumped. He sank, clawed to the top of the swirling water and struck out for the deadly, churning legs of the stallion. Too close and he'd be knocked into eternity.

Three feet from the muzzle of the stallion, Wash treaded water, pulled his knife from its boot pocket. Then grabbing the loose end of his rope but leaving a nine foot length attached to the noose, he cut it.

Now Briley's rope pulled the horse away and Wash could swim to him from the side. That long black mane, he needed to . . . he grabbed for it, twined his fingers into its matted mass and with a kick and a heave pulled himself onto the back of the sinking stallion.

"Loose my rope!" Briley yelled.

Barely able to keep his nose above the surface of the water, the stallion struck out for the far side. Wash slid his hand under Briley's noose and with the help of the water floated it off the horse's head. Frantically, he grabbed his own rope as he felt the first heave of those iron legs scrabbling for a hold on the rocky bottom.

A violent snort, a shake of his head, and the stallion was stumbling up the bank, around the cut and into the open.

Wash could hear Briley's laugh and hoorah as he began the wildest ride of his life.

Chapter Nineteen

Wash clung to the back of the mustang with locked knees, one hand grasping the long mane, the other wound into the middle of the noose rope, letting the end trail the ground on one side. *How long can he run?* Wash wondered. *How long can I hold on?*

Several times the stallion tried to buck him off, kicking out with his hind quarters while still running. When he could not unseat his tenacious rider he tried biting, flipping his head around, nipping the nearest leg. He finally succeeded at this. He tore a plug out of Wash's right calf, nearly unseating him. But Wash hung on, as determined as the horse not to lose this fight.

The sun had set, the early night sky was streaked with pink. The evening star was out. Still the stubborn little mustang ran.

They had gone through flat prairies, over sand beds, into stands of cedar and cactus. The ochre-colored horse was dark with mud and sweat. His nostrils, flared wide to catch the wind, were bleeding. He had stumbled once onto gravel and his knees oozed blood.

"You'll die, you cussed animal," Wash cried, his hands rubbed raw, his knees weak as a newborn colt.

Finally they came to one of the side creeks of the Yellow Cat. "It's time to end this," Wash mumbled. Shouting 'whoas' intermingled with jerks on the rope and pressure on his thighs, he drove the mustang into the shallow creekbed. The water was a foot deep, putting a drag onto the tired legs of the stallion.

Wash looked ahead. Just what he needed. The creek suddenly came to a stop, the embankment in front of them was over four feet steep and sand-slippery. "You'll not go up that, you muleheaded bronc," Wash panted. He was exhausted. His hands were bleeding now, his legs trembling.

Before the dun could turn, Wash slid off his back, stumbling backward into the creek. Here the water was only inches deep over gravel and sand. Finding his balance, Wash stood up straight in the middle of the channel, daring the stallion to go past him.

The horse whirled around, snorted, pawed the damp earth, struck out with one hoof and knocked Wash to the ground. "Darn you, horse!" Wash countered. "If I had my gun I'd shoot you."

In answer the mustang bared his teeth and struck. Wash jumped up and stumbled out of range, swatting at him like a fly. "Not again you don't," he yelled, glancing down at his bleeding leg.

Hot and sweating from anger and fear, the stallion turned round and round, not wanting to tackle the steep embankment yet unable to pass the man.

With one eye on the confused animal, Wash slowly

bent to pick up the end of the rope that dragged the ground. Swiftly he flicked the end, hitting the dun's face. The startled mustang whinnied and reared up. Again, Wash flicked the rope. The dun turned and made for the embankment. But his hooves could gain no foothold and he tumbled onto his back with a screeching whistle.

"I hope your back's broke," Wash said through gritted teeth. Before the horse could regain his footing, Wash jumped in and flicked the rope into the startled dun's eyes. He grunted, tried to bite, missed, and with a lunge flopped upright where he stood trembling, groaning like some wounded bear. Wash hit him again on the nose. The dun shook, then dropped his head.

"Now maybe you're ready, you son of a gun," Wash wailed, rubbing his leg. He waited, hoping indeed the horse was ready. He was. The dun dropped his head lower, then lifted it slowly. Turning aside, he began licking his lips, bobbing his head up and down, licking his lips.

"All right!" Wash breathed a sigh. "It's about time." It was working. The tired horse was asking for relief. He wanted no more. He would accept Wash as master.

"Whoa boy," Wash tried to put a hum in his voice all the while wishing he could throttle the critter. Why had Briley put him up to this stunt?

"This is where it ends. You and me are gonna be partners . . . yea, ha ha." He was breathing as hard as the stallion whose legs were also trembling. "It's a matter of me now being boss," he said, straining to put a gentlness in his tone. The subdued horse stood listening and when Wash was satisfied with his subdued stance, Wash turned sideways to the horse. Then he turned his back and waited.

In a moment the dun snorted. Wash could feel his heat. He could feel his wet breath, then he could feel the stallion's soft nose as it nuzzled his back.

Wash grinned with relief. Keeping the rope loosely trailing between them, he began to walk ahead of the dun, leading him down the creekbed.

Together they walked out of the water onto the dry shore and under a copse of willows. The horse blew out, danced away, but did not threaten to run or to fight.

Wash pulled a hobbling string from his back pocket and stooping, being careful of those fidgety front hooves, managed to tie them together.

Then his own legs collapsed and he dropped onto the weedy grass and closed his eyes. He couldn't believe it. Briley's impossible plan had worked. His hands burned, his chest felt as if it would never get enough air, and he was so weak he could not get up if the stallion broke the hobbles.

Instantly he was asleep.

Chapter Twenty

Briley pulled his hat down tighter on his head. A wind had kicked up after he left the hills and the sky was awhirl with sand and blowing leaves. "Gonna be a doozy," he told the grulla. "Let's git ourselves on into town and see thet girl."

Smoke Rising was closing the huge front double doors when Briley rode inside. "Thank'e miss," he acknowledged with a toss of his head.

The wind blew a gully-wash of heavy rain against the wooden doors. Smoke Rising bolted them shut then wiped her wet face with her sleeve. "There's a stall," she said, nodding toward the last one on their right. I'll get water. Do you want grain?"

Briley slapped his sopping hat against a leg and asked, "Are you the girl they call Smoke Risin'?" The girl was small, her long hair dark with curls that fell onto her forehead. She had a black eye and a swollen cheek.

She stopped, looked at the old man who was a

stranger. Slowly she said, "Yes, I'm Smoke Rising. Who are you?"

Briley ambled toward the back of the stable, glancing into the shadows thrown off by the lanterns hanging on the stall posts. Horses were standing asleep or lying on haybeds, or hanging their heads over their gates hoping for attention.

The back door was propped half-open with a bucket of water. Briley stuck his head outside, squinting into the alley.

"Leave that open," the girl called in a loud voice. "We need air."

"Anyone else here?" Briley asked.

Smoke Rising picked up one of the pitch forks. "What do you want, Mister?"

Briley stared at the girl. Her eyes were like a caught rabbit's, dark with fear, yet bright with planning her escape. Was she Wash Buchanan's woman?

Briley rubbed the nose of the grulla and said, "Sorry Miss, but I have something to tell you and it'd be better if no one else heard it."

"What is it?" She was curt. He realized she was still afraid. Strange, under the flickering light from the lanterns, she reminded him of someone. But of course he'd never seen her before. "Wash Buchanan says to tell you he's alive."

Smoke Rising swayed, stuck the pitchfork in the ground and leaned on it. "You." She looked down at his boots. They were worn and lop-sided. "You're the one at the gorge."

"Yep. How'd you know thet?"

A sudden gust of wind banged the back door shut, overturning the bucket. Then blew it open again. One of the horses whinnied and stomped in his stall. The grulla's ears shot forward.

Smoke Rising glanced that way, then in a minute turned back to Briley. "I rode out the next day and saw . . . Hoshaba. I found your tracks and I saw the grave. What about the grave?"

"Jis for looks. Hopin' to stall them Whelpers from knowing the feller wus still alive."

"Where is he? Is he all right?"

"He's hid good, don't worry. And he's all right. Didn't want to live when he saw thet horse's legs—I had to shoot it you know—but Buchanan come around."

Smoke Rising put a fist to her mouth. She did not want to cry. "I . . . I need to tell him I'm sorry I left him that day. I shouldn't have. Please, let me see him."

"Not now, Miss. You stay here and do your chores so's he won't worry none. And don't spread it about him bein' alive."

"No. No, I won't. Tell him . . . oh, does he need anything?"

"Nope. I'll take care o' his needs fer a spell. But say," he scratched his head and added, "Whut do you know 'bout this Whelper? He do thet to you?"

Smoke Rising put a finger on her cheek. Her look changed. When she said "Yes", Briley felt that old anger rising anew in his chest. Jack Whelper's just like his father, he thought. Taking a woman by force when it can't be had any other way.

Smoke Rising seemed glad to tell what she knew. "Whelper has hired guns, you saw them if you watched them chase Wash over the gorge. Whelper and his brother claim land from the Platte all the way to Fort Laramie. There's a line cabin somewhere near Big Hole and he sells cattle regularly, likely stolen. Other ranches have lost heavily but no one dares accuse him."

"Well, don't worry none, Whelper'll be took care of." He stopped, "Oh yea, thet boy could use some o' his clothes. If you could git to his room at the hotel we'd be obliged."

"Yes. Yes I can. Where would I leave them?"

"You know his grandpa's place?"

"Yes. I'll leave them there. Thank you, Mister . . . ?"

"I'm called Briley, Ma'am. Well, I'll be goin'."

The rain was steady, falling straight from the sky. Smoke Rising opened one of the front doors. Briley touched his hat and rode out.

The back door closed as Smoke Rising bolted the front one.

Stoop Ragan grinned when he slipped into the alley.

Briley stopped for a drink at the Drovers. He'd not had a saloon drink in ten years. He was certain no one knew him, not even the Whelpers. He'd changed in all those years and besides, they were not interested in him now that they had Buchanan.

He ordered a beer, but when he looked around he knew something was wrong. The saloon was nearly vacant. A lone man played solitaire at one of the tables. He raised his eyes to glare at Briley, then, uninterested, slapped down another card.

Clem leaned close as he set a warm beer in front of Briley. "Where is everone?" Briley asked in a low mumble. His hackles were up.

Clem motioned with a tilt of his head and mumbled through a tight mouth, "New gun in town. He shot one o' Delight's young hands. It's run all my customers off. He'll be leavin' soon though to side for Jack Whelper."

The beer caught in Briley's throat and he sputtered into his hand. "Yea . . . well, thanks," he managed and, easing out of his chair, he left the Drovers.

Outside, he mounted the mustang and rode for awhile with his backside itching. Covered by the darkness, he soon settled into a slumbering trot, certain the gunman had not followed.

Briley didn't mind the rain. As soon as he got to the Sand Flats he'd bed down under his tarp and sleep like a baby.

But the grulla was edgy, kept looking to the side, flapping his ears back and forth. "You tryin' to tell me somethin', boy?" Briley mumbled.

When lightning flashed, Briley whirled around in the saddle. A rider was lit up on his right flank. Not carrying a rifle, keeping back, but close. It was Stoop Ragan for sure. That paint horse was like a sign with his name on it.

"A ignert tracker if I ever saw one," Briley informed the grulla. "Could'a shot me long ago."

So what did he want? Then Briley remembered the slamming door at the livery. *Darn! Ragan was the wind that opened that back door. Now Whelper'll know Buchanan is alive. And if he follows me, he'll find the cabin.*

Briley went west, the rain would cover his tracks if he could outmaneuver the man. There were rocks and gravel pits near the Sand Flats and he headed for those, but in a roundabout way.

Slipping in and out of tree stands, brushes, and gullies, waiting behind a hump in the path, then putting the mustang into a run, he soon lost his tail. The rain did the rest.

By the time he got past the flats he was ready to bed

down. He laid out his tarp under a rock ledge with his back to the rock and hunkered close inside.

Yep, Briley reassured himself. If the man following wanted to kill him he'd already have done it before they left town or soon after. That left only one reason for trailing him . . . he wanted Briley to lead him to Buchanan.

Before day, Briley crawled out from his tarp and mounted a wet saddle. He checked his back trail. No tracks, either his or any others. He turned north, headed not for the cabin, but for that line camp of Whelper's near Big Hole.

Chapter Twenty-one

Wash woke with the sun in his eyes. He rolled to one side, searching for the dun. Would he still be here? He was. He stood cropping the short dry grass not twenty yards away.

Wash stumbled to his feet. Blazes, he was stiff. That trick yesterday had nearly killed him. Now to get the stallion back to the pool and find his supplies.

It was only as difficult as a half-tamed, still mean critter could make it. The stallion reached for Wash's arm with his teeth bared. Wash slapped his muzzle and flipped the rope into his eyes. "You'll learn yet," he said and leaped onto his back.

After a five minute tussle during which the dun again tried to unseat Wash, he quieted down and they began to walk, then trot, then gallop.

In an hour Wash was back at the watering pool, looking for the beans and flour Briley said he would leave. This time he not only hobbled the dun, he put the leather halter on him that he found in the packs and tied it with a long rope to a tree. The stallion could eat and drink as he pleased. Or starve, for all Wash cared.

Wash set beans to cook for his evening meal then opened a can of tomatoes which he ate with biscuits and jerky. He made a pot of strong coffee and drank half of it.

Then he began to practice with the .45. Since Briley had first shown him, he had worked with the gun every chance he got but he needed more practice if he expected to hedge out the Whelpers.

He went a thousand yards away from the dun. When the horse seemed accustomed to the sound from that distance he came closer and fired. Then closer again until he was ten feet from the stallion without it doing anything but making him flinch and look up each time.

That night Wash soaked his right hand in hot salt water. He had blisters not only from the ride but from the pistol shooting.

The next day he let his hand rest in the morning. In the afternoon he practiced until he could flip the gun out of the holster and fire it in one swift movement as Briley had done.

Several times during the day he worked with the stallion. Each time he kept himself from being bitten or stomped by sheer speed of movement. "Got your wind back have you?" Wash stated as he wrangled the bit between the clenched teeth.

He threw the saddle he'd used with Hoshaba onto the mustang's back and tried to cinch it. That disturbed the dun, but using lots of patience and some soothing words—which he didn't really mean—Wash got the cinch tightened and stepped on board.

The dun kicked and twirled. Soon realizing it was no use, he allowed himself to be led, turned, stopped, booted into a long, hard, working gallop.

That night it rained. Sitting under a shed of cedar boughs with his face to a spitting fire, Wash studied the horse. He stood under a low-limbed cedar not ten feet away, highlighted by the flames. "You are one rough critter," Wash told him. "Briley said you wore scars on your neck and shoulders. He didn't begin to tell the tale. You must have riled a mountain cat."

Wash stirred the fire brighter as he tried to assess the confirmation he knew the finest thoroughbreds should possess. As Hoshaba possessed. He laughed as he measured by eye the dun's neck and shoulder slope, the withers, the legs, backside and frontside. Nothing stood the test. The dun was nobble-kneed, short-necked, with a stubby body and a pair of crooked, mismatched, laid-back ears. What a mess you are for a horse, Wash decided. And mean as the devil to boot.

Then the vision of Hoshaba filled the night and Wash felt like a traitor. "You'll never take his place you ugly cuss. If I didn't need you I'd cut you free right now."

Chapter Twenty-two

Wash was at the cabin three days after his wild ride. Briley was unloading Asa. "Got grub here," Briley proudly announced. "A hunk o' smoked venison, salt bacon, and rice—ever eat rice? And lookie here. This here is pickled peaches. Got all this from an old lady name o' Witcomb. Wus passin' her place and she welcomed to sell me from her goods. I gave her a twenty dollar gold piece. You think thet's too much?"

Wash studied the glistening red peaches nestled in thick syrup in a glass jar. "Nope, you didn't pay too much.

"But Briley, did you see Smoke Rising?"

Briley cut himself a plug and shook his head. "Saw her and told her. Said she wus mighty sorry she left you alone thet day . . . but . . . well it's not good, Buchanan. We wus overheard whilst I wus tellin' her. He followed me without shootin' me down when he could. Recognized Stoop Ragan's pinto."

Wash sighed. "That's too bad. Did you shake him?"

"Oh yea. He don't know where we're at except he may ask around and come up with the where-o-bouts of this here cabin."

"We could have used another week without them knowing. Now we'd better get busy. I'll visit the ranches between my place and Whelper's on the east. See if any of those spreads are missing cattle and if the owners will testify."

Briley began to pack food along with a small skillet and a tin can for coffee into a leather saddle-pack. "You'll need grub." He glanced at Wash's pants and added, "Thet girl says she'll leave some o' your clothes at your place. Looks like you'll need 'em. Whut happened?"

Wash stuck his finger in the hole of his pants. "That dang horse. Bit a plug out of my leg, bit my arm, my hand, stomped me in the ground. He's a mean bugger."

Briley chuckled as he glanced at the tied dun. "But you got him, by jiggers. How'd you ride him so quick?"

I've learned about gentling wild broncs since I was a tad. My uncle taught me. This one still wants to put you in your place though."

"Then why don't he?" Briley frowned. He had spent a month busting the grulla.

"Because he had to give up and ask me for mercy. When he did that then I became the leader. He just doesn't like it."

Briley finished pouring flour into a small leather pouch, then he stuffed it into one side of a double saddle-pack. "Here's your grub stake. And Buchanan, I took a turn by a place thet gal mentioned. Whelper has a line shack near Big Hole—here, let me show you." He took a stick and drew in the dirt. "No one wus there but it's been a busy place times past. There's a set o' holdin' pens big enough to work a few steers, yet not big enough to keep a hundert beeves such as Whelper ships at one time.

"And somethin' else strange, Buchanan, fer this here country. No sign of a brandin' fire ever been built around thet place and no irons anywheres. I took me a peek in the shack and in the barn shed. So my guess is, Whelper is stashing and brandin' his stolen beeves somewheres else."

"Yes, that has to be. After I take a look at our neighbors I'll check out the country on the other side of his place. In the meantime you watch out for Smoke. I don't like leaving her alone to fend off Whelper."

Briley glanced up with hooded eyes.

"What's the matter? You know something?"

Briley spat hard. "Yea. Thet girl, Smoke Risin', wus sportin' a black eye and bruise on her pretty face. Tol me herself Jack Whelper did it."

"Curse the man!" Wash cried and slung the small hatchet he was about to pack into a nearby tree. "I'm ready. Let's go."

Chapter Twenty-three

For two sultry days Wash urged the dun through the rough back country of three of the smaller ranches that drove cattle to the rail at Granite. None of these had barbed wire and Wash wondered if Drennan was not having the luck he claimed in selling the stuff.

Wash had seen a few outlaw steers and a cow with her calf but no real herds. He decided to drop south enough to hit his own place. See if Smoke had left him any of his clothes.

He had no doubt Whelper was staying away from the Ross spread. The man was too smart to be hanging around there.

Wash rode easy over his ranch, enjoying the feel of owning land and trees and water. Ha! even the birds and field grouse belonged to him . . . at least as much as any land or game belonged to a man.

The dun proved tireless and was satisfied with sparse grass or even weeds and tree leaves. His walk was choppy, but when he broke into his lope or faster run he was as smooth as Hoshaba.

Rain threatened with an overlay of dirty clouds holding in the heat. Wash's shirt clung to him, his whole body was sticky, and his legs itched inside the filthy, torn pants.

Thunder growled along the horizon accompanied by slender spikes of silver lightning. He reined the mustang under a tiny drip-shed just as it began to rain. The old house was a welcome shelter and he ducked quickly inside. He shook off water and looked around with a funny feeling crawling up his neck . . . as if he were an intruder. Could this ever be his home? He wondered.

Ignoring the paltry-furnished front room he went directly to the bedroom where he immediately found his clothes. It felt good to get out of the blood-soaked, dirty pants and the shirt he'd worn for the last week. And new socks soothed his burning feet. Too bad his boots were beginning to look like old Briley's.

When his eye fell on the book he grinned. Smoke had thought to put it in the bundle. His hand reached automatically for *The Talisman* . . . that book of his childhood he'd shared so intimately with his father.

Sitting on the creaky bed next to the window, he began to read the story of the gallant knight who risked life and personal honor for his country. Wash thought of his father and wondered how he had felt taking up arms as he did, when he wanted only to teach and to be with his son and wife. "Times never change, people never learn, do they, Pa?" Wash whispered as he laid the book under the scarf in the drawer that had once been his mother's.

* * *

The mustang was nervous, shied at the least sound.

A deep slope carried them into a coulee, only a little soggy and full of thistles, but with another downpour it could be a deathtrap of rushing water. Here he came upon a good number of older stock. He rode close to a steer and read the brand, a little L inside a big D. A chuck wagon was parked around a hillock and he rode up. Three hands were standing at a branding fire, one brandished a rifle, his stance a warning. Wash asked if they had trouble losing cattle. They shook their heads, saying their boss would have to answer that.

Early afternoon, Wash found the owner. The dun threw up his head and snorted. A rider came out of the draw in front of Wash holding a pointed gun. Wash had a time holding the mustang in check.

The rider was a young, sun-browned man wearing a rainslick. "You're trespassin' I guess you know," he bellowed out loud and clear.

"Like to talk," Wash answered.

"Talk."

Wash eased the dun to within a few feet of the man and when the gun was lowered he explained who he was and what he wanted. The man listened but he would not help. His name was Delight and he had kept a close watch the past year on his stock. Had cut his losses from the year before.

"Done had enough trouble without askin' for it. Lost one o' my men just a few days ago to one of Whel . . . well, to a gun-happy cuss in town. If I started complaining to that wheeze-basket of a sheriff, he'd probably hang *me*."

Wash swiped a hand through his hair and replaced his

hat. "I saw that happen, Delight. And it was a killing for no call. But we can't let such keep happening."

Delight clicked his mount. "Can't help now, Buchcnan, and you'll do well to turn tracks and leave off this detective stuff. Round here, cattle just disappear into thin air, leaving no wounded stuff behind and no cold branding fires or dead steers. Only thing I ever found wus a shot calf. No one's gonna catch any rustlers in this country."

"Who's next to you?" Wash asked, feeling things closing down. Everyone was afraid.

"Crowder ranges next door but he'll sure be no help. He's run into Whelper once't already about lost cattle and paid for it. He's right backward, a family man who works his two growed sons and they don't see by strangers."

"Well, thanks for listening, Delight, but I'll mosey on over anyway. Maybe Crowder will change his mind."

Wash rode five miles before dropping into a deep arroyo. The dun suddenly stopped, wouldn't budge. He lifted his nose as if to smell the air. "I'll be," Wash muttered, "If you're not sniffing like a hound. What is it?"

Wash dismounted and by straining on the reins managed to pull the stallion to the center of a roughed out depression. "Well, well," he mused. "What have we here?"

The dead coals of a fire were scattered about. In the middle, inside the ashes, lay part of a carcass. Wash bent on one knee to examine the remains of a good sized steer. The edible parts had been hacked out, the rest left for the vultures.

He noticed one large hunk still had the hide intact and

when he moved it he could see the brand. It was a big "C." "No range owner would kill one of his best steers and leave half of it," he muttered and then remembered something. That first day when he had overheard Whelper's hands, one was saying a W could cover a big C "right well" . . . merely seeming to be a crooked W.

This steer had been a meal for rustlers! And not too long ago.

Wash stood up, studying the layout.

Suddenly the lineback quivered and jumped back. Wash felt a low rumble in the earth. Cattle moving. Fast. And close by.

Wash coaxed the horse away from the dead fire to a place among heavy bushes. He tied him, then inched up the side of the caprock to the level plateau. He had a good view and he estimated the bunch of beeves to be about one-hundred fifty. They were being hard-driven by three cowboys. He recognized one as the man he had jumped at the rail station.

These were Whelper's cowboys. They were putting together a bunch of Crowder cattle and leaving a good trail. He would give them time, then follow. Wash felt a rush of excitement. He was soon going to find the place Whelper held his stolen beeves.

Hurrying, he scooted down the hill to the dead steer, then started toward the tied dun when he heard, "Drop the gun, Mister, and turn 'round." The thick-tongued voice was hot with anger.

Wash's skin tingled as he eased the Colt out and dropped it. He turned and looked up into the eyes of three hulking figures.

Crowder and his two sons were taller than Wash, well over six feet three, and squinty-eyed edgy. Wash had a time telling the father from the sons. They were all of the same ilk, hard-dryed filthy. They reeked of unwashed clothes and bodies of at least a winter's standing. Whether the old man had wrinkles was impossible to tell under the layers of soot and sour sweat.

"Git it, Otis Dell."

The one carrying a '73 Winchester grinned a fat-cat grin and picked up the Colt.

"Naow," their father continued to drawl, "We got us a thieven Whelper at last. Caught red-handed having jus killed a Crowder steer."

"This steer was killed hours ago," Wash said steadily. "The fire is out, ashes are cold. And I didn't do it. Your cattle are being sto. . . ."

The old man struck Wash across the mouth with his rifle butt.

Wash had flinched when he saw the hit coming and it saved him a broken jaw. But he fell with the blow and lay stunned.

When he could see straight he raised up on one elbow and growled, "I'm not a Whelper man, I'm trailing them. I want to catch Whelper and his bunch as much as you. My name is Wash Buchanan. I've come here to get your help." Wash felt his words drop on unbelieving ears and the darkness of the coming storm suddenly seemed menacing.

He limped to his feet expecting another blow but the three men hunched forward, watching him. "Look, the four of us have a chance of getting your beeves back. They just crossed that ravine to the north. I saw them. Please. . . ."

"We done tried thet, Mister," Crowder stated coldly, glancing at one of his sons. "Got our stock back and run off them renegades in a hell o' fire." He sucked air like a kid about to cry then blurted out, "And Whelper dry-gulched Joe Paul the nex day."

A grip of silence settled on them all. Then Wash tried, "It'll be different this time, I'll. . . ."

"Nope. Harlin, fetch a rope."

At the word rope, Wash spun around, kicking an ancient .44 out of Harlin's hand. Wash went scrambling after it on his hands and knees. A bizarre yell sailed up from Otis Dell who flung the .45 and his Winchester aside and leaped on Wash like a crazed wildcat. The two-hundred-fifty pound hulk flattened Wash face—down into the dirt. His nose spurted blood as the heavens burst apart. Rain began to fall in a deluge.

Water and blood ran from Wash's nose, soaking his shirt. He tried to run, was pulled down by a red-eyed Harlin. Wash could see old man Crowder watching the fray, evidently hoping his sons would make the rope unnecessary.

A fist from out of the slushy blackness connected with Wash's face and the dirty knuckle split his cheek. Wash grabbed a patch of long gritty hair and swung a low, deliberate crack into its owner's face.

Otis Dell whimpered and slumped over.

Harlin picked up the Winchester, holding it like a club, ready for a round-house swing. Wash sucked in his belly and felt the swish of the rifle as it careened by. This was foolish, he decided. He was not their enemy. Anger at it all put the force of a mule behind his boot as he followed the rifle thrust with a kick into the huge man's gut, doubling him over, sending him sliding into the mud with a soft, spewing sound.

"That'll be all now," their father entoned. "Git over to that tree." Pointing a shotgun at Wash he nodded toward a tall pine. "Now you boys see if you're able to find your guns and help me tie up this here thief."

Chapter Twenty-four

Wash shivered as the night temperature dropped and his fighting blood quieted. The cut on his cheek stung and his head ached. The way his head was tied forced the rain to fall off his forehead into his eyes.

The Crowders were arguing. Otis Dell punctuated his vote to "hang the buzzard now" with trips over to the pine so that Wash could get the full import of his wishes.

Wash doubted Harlin cared which course they took and he just hoped ole man Crowder had enough sense to prevent a lynching.

The rain was steady, coming down in a black sheet of drowning dispair. The Crowders didn't seem to mind. They walked about without hat or coat and had no preference for the tarp one of them had strung between a rope and a tree.

They drank from a bottle Harlin removed from his pack and after a while Otis went off into the night. Sometime later he drove up with a wagon hitched to a team of lank mules. A grub sack was thrown down and they argued and cussed as they cooked something in a squatty black pot.

Wash tried to loosen the ropes during the times they were in a hot discussion, but the ropes were tied so tight they cut circulation. His feet were already numb. As the night wore on Wash drifted into a semi-sleep only to choke on the rope as his head fell. The fire and men became a weird dance of shadows and flickering light and he was on the outside in the cold.

When the argument ceased the ole man came over and whacked his shotgun against Wash's boot.

"You wake?"

Wash stared.

"Kids won out. We're tired o' you renegades stealin' and gittin' away with it. We'll wait til morning though . . . maybe it'll clear."

"To do what?" Wash gurgled.

"Hang ya, Mister. From this here tree."

The rain slackened before dawn and turned to a fine peppery mist. The tree had been a slight shelter but Wash was drenched and soggy-cold. He had pulled and chewed on his hand ropes til his gums bled but the ropes would not give.

Surprisingly, he had spotted his Colt on a ridge of grass within fifteen feet of the tree, where it had been kicked during the fight. It may as well have been a mile away.

Wash rehearsed his argument, going over in his mind the facts he could present that these people might give him a reprieve. But he knew he was fooling himself. They were not prone to listen to reason, they were frightened and ignorant and wanted revenge. Same as he did.

Except they had the wrong man.

The sound of a rider made Wash's heart stir and he strained to see who it was. The men were asleep in the wagon. One crawled out and went up to the rider. They spoke in inaudible tones. Whoever it was was small, maybe a woman dressed in pants. He tossed a package to the men and they fell on it like animals.

Out came a slab of bacon and the Crowders built up the fire and began cutting and frying and whooping.

The stranger joined them in eating the bacon and they talked and ate and drank whiskey. Wash saw them looking in his direction and the rider left the fire and came over. He pulled up ten feet away staring, then ran to the tree and fell on his knees. It was no woman but a boy.

"Mr. Buchanan?" the boy asked half in recognition half in wonder. Wash frowned through the watery haze trying to place the voice.

"Gee. . . ." the slight figure marveled at Wash's appearance. "I'm Lester . . . the boy from the hotel, Mr. Buchanan. You got it agin didn't you. Pa thinks you're a Whelper."

Wash expressed a tired "huh."

"Pa's pretty upset. Thinks you were in with the rustlers who've been stealin' his cattle."

"He's wrong."

"Yea, I know, but Pa's set on it. See, lass year they killed my brother, and well . . . Pa's not gonna be happy with lettin' you go."

"But you can tell him who I am." Wash lifted his tied hands.

"Wouldn't do no good Mr. Buchanan. Pa makes up his mind, it's against his Code to change it."

"Code?" Wash tried to swallow and couldn't.

"His Code of a Righteous Man. He never breaks it . . . it's his word. Once it's made."

"This isn't breaking a man's word, Lester. This is ac . . . accepting facts."

"Not to Pa." The boy glanced at the fire and the men around it. "That's why Ma and me live in town. She couldn't bide by his ways and up and left and took me with her.

"But I come out ever Sunday."

"This is Sunday?" Wash felt defeated as he thought of the time gone by. "Boy, can you untie me?"

When the boy lowered his head Wash said gently, "He'd whip you, huh?"

"Not just that but he'd never let me come on the ranch agin . . . and he's promised me a new Colt, and. . . ."

"Okay, son. Look, you can do this though and they'll never be sure about it. Get me my gun. It's right over there by that hump. Left there after the fight. I'll tell them it was close enough for me to work it over with my feet."

The boy nodded okay, then went back to the fire, commenting on the luck of catching a Whelper.

It was easy to get the gun. The boy fooled around the camp like a boy would, stubbing his toe at gopher mounds, hunting for a good branch to "make him something." He picked up the Colt and carried it with his sticks over to the tree where he wrangled loudly about no-good outlaws. He dropped the Colt six inches beside Wash's hip.

Crowder decided Lester was too young to see the hanging and sent him home. Otis Dell sat in the wagon rolling and tying the hanging knot. Harlin went to get their horses they'd staked in a nearby patch of grass.

Crowder walked up. "Say your prayers, Mister." His

tongue was drugged with whiskey and he swayed on his feet. Wash lifted the wrist-breaking .45 from between his legs and lined it up with the middle button on Crowder's dingy wet underwear.

"Take out your knife and cut these ropes," Wash said slowly and clearly. "And be real particular about it. I don't want to blow a hole in that highly-treasured pair of longjohns."

Wash had to hand it to the old man. He scratched and swayed and broke out in a grin. "That gun been out in the rain. It ain't 'bout to fire."

"Maybe. You willing to chance it?" Otis was still working with the rope, but for how long? And Harlin could drive up any minute.

Crowder took out a pocket knife and flipped it open. The handle was grubby but the blade was newly honed. It cut the ropes in one tug.

Wash gripped the gun with tingling fingers and inched his way up the tree to lean against it. His legs stung.

"Now call Otis Dell over here and do it natural like."

The man called out and had to ask twice before his older son responded. Wash prayed he'd be able to stand long enough to give orders. "Sit," he demanded and watched the dumbfounded expression on Otis Dell's face as he eased to the ground.

Wash told Crowder to bind his son's feet and hands, then remove both their boots and tie his own feet.

Backing off, Wash kept the Colt on the man's chest until he reached the Winchester propped against the wagon. Just then Harlin came in view and Crowder and Otis began hollering.

But Wash leveled the rifle at Harlin and growled a command for him to sit and tie his own feet.

Wash's feet and legs felt like a million ants stinging all at once, he didn't know if he could keep standing, but he gathered the boots, threw them into the wagon, and pulled himself into the driver's seat. He "hyahed" and slapped the reins over the mules.

The men were quarreling and cursing as Wash took off toward the grove of bushes where he'd tied the dun late yesterday. It would be a miracle if he were still there.

Maybe Wash deserved a little special help because the mustang was there, drooping and wet. He tossed his ugly head at sight of Wash and the mules, nickering a warning welcome.

As quickly as his aching hands and feet would allow, Wash stepped into the rain-slippery saddle and clicked the mustang up the draw, slugging through the muddy seep to higher ground.

Chapter Twenty-five

A tapping on her door brought a cold chill to Smoke Rising. How much longer could she hold off Jack Whelper? That thrashing he'd taken in the livery must have shaken his pride. He'd not stand very long being bested by a woman.

Her hand crept under the edge of her mattress and drew out a knife. She sat up, pulling a blanket over her breast to cover the weapon. "Who is it?" she asked.

"It's Briley, Miss." The deep whisper relaxed the tightness in her body. She padded to the door and cracking it, motioned him in.

"Waited til night to come," he explained. "Didn't care none to be noticed." Seeing her question he added, "I followed you here from the stable. You still want to help Buchanan?"

"Yes. How is he?"

"He's okay. Out scoutin' for evidence of Whelper's rustlin'. We split. I went back of Whelper land to the

Big Hole. Found a line cabin there where he works his stolen cattle. But it's not big enough for more'n fifty at a time so he has another place somewheres. You happen to know where that might be?"

Smoke Rising shook her head. "No. Jack is very careful what he says around me . . . or anybody." She frowned. "Do you know what danger you're in, Briley?"

"Don't matter. What we need is to get the law out here. Buchanan won't cotton to shootin' first and askin' questions later. He wants it all nice and legal-like. We need to get a telegram to that marshall in Cheyenne. One that'll rouse his mind to git in the saddle. Buchanan tried, but I figure his telegram never got sent."

"I don't know if my word would . . . wait. Elizabeth Drennan could get a telegram through. And her word and her father's would count with any law man."

"Wash mentioned that gal so I reckon it'll be safe to let her in on this. We need him here in three days. If he's not here by then we'll take care o' Whelper on our own."

"Oh . . . I'm glad someone finally has the guts to stand up to that man." She touched his arm. "Take care, Briley. It isn't settled yet."

As Briley stepped outside he looked back at the closed door. That girl, the way she put out her hand and touched him just like Mary Rose would've done. . . . Darn, he was getting too old for this.

Wash's nose was swollen. The hole the dun bit out of his leg throbbed. His cheek was bleeding, it would probably get infected from that dirty knuckle. His hands and feet were cold and numb. "We gotta find a resting place," Wash muttered. "Somewhere out of this mucky rain."

He was off the Crowder spread but he'd not turned south. He was headed north. If those stolen cattle had been bedded down during the rain maybe he'd be able to find tracks. But first he needed to sleep.

He said this to the dun then slumped in the saddle, letting go of the reins. Wherever the mustang wanted to go was all right with him.

Thirty minutes later Wash jerked awake. They were under the ledge of one of those granite boulders, its overhang keeping the floor dry in the cave-like room. "Thanks," Wash muttered, never doubting for a moment that this crazy horse could understand English.

"You first," he said, pulling off the wet saddle. He tossed it aside then noticed the stems and brittle dead leaves of choke—weed growing up under the ledge. He plucked a handful of the leaves and began rubbing the dun's dripping neck and sides.

At the first touch, the dun whipped his head around with his teeth bared. That open mouth got one inch from Wash's arm then the teeth clamped shut. Wash kept rubbing, too weary to care whether he got bit or not, and the mustang dropped his head and closed his eyes.

There was grain in one of the pouches and Wash poured it into a hollow on the rock floor. The dun had never eaten grain. He nosed it around, finally licking it, then scooping it up into his mouth and contentedly chewing.

Wash Buchanan had never had to fend for himself under these conditions. City life had called for no such endeavors. But he knew he needed food and rest. " 'Nature has her demands for refreshment and repose, even on the iron frame. . . .', says the Couchant Knight," Wash solemnly told the dun. And he began to make a small fire out of the dry weedy limbs.

Next he poured water from his canteen into the tin can, added coffee grounds and set it atop the flame. He ate a biscuit and a handful of dried apples. He chewed on some jerky, waiting for the coffee to boil.

He found a rag in his pack, wet it in the rain falling from the ledge and wiped the blood from his face. Then he rolled his blanket out of the rainslick he'd never untied, and lay down.

He fell into a deep sleep.

When he woke the cave was hazy-dark and someone was standing over him, a great black shadow of a being. Wash's mouth went dry. He would never reach his gun, or the knife in his boot. He turned his head slightly toward the entrance light, hoping to recognize who it was.

When he did, he slumped into his blanket, weak as a mewling kitten. You son of a gun, he thought to himself, not daring to disturb the sleeping mustang too quickly. He snuffled and shifted position. The dun blinked, then swung his head away from hanging over Wash Buchanan's body.

Wash eased himself up and sat for a moment with a tightness swelling in his throat. "You keeping watch, huh?" he said and reached up to touch the dun's dark muzzle. To Wash's astonishment it quivered. It was as soft and vulnerable as Hoshaba's. Wash ran a light finger down the rib of one of the deep, ragged scars. "What happened?" he whispered. "Whatever it was was bad, huh, fellow? You'n me are the same, aren't we boy, having our troubles, needing each other like we do."

The rain had stopped. Wash drank cold coffee, ate another biscuit, and spent time cleaning, even firing the

.45. With a grim face he holstered the pistol then mounted the dun with his nose pointed toward the hills where Crowder's rustled cattle were headed.

The terrain changed during midday. It was now starkly barren, dotted with rocks and hills. Wash was no tracker, and any hoof prints had been obliterated during the night's rain. He wished he had Briley with him. He wondered what the old man was doing. Had he found the marshall? Was Smoke all right?

"Let's go west awhile," he told the dun and reined that way. "Maybe I misjudged and they drove the beeves *around* this rough country, not through it. If they did, then they'd be up yonder way and we should pick up new, morning-made tracks. That is, if they bedded during the night."

He kicked the stallion into a lope.

He found the tracks as the sun inched toward the west horizon. They cut in front of him from the east and were headed into that mountainous area between his own spread and Whelper's—those rocky buttes he'd asked Smoke Rising about. *Where in the world will this lead?* he wondered.

He pulled his carbine from the boot. He wasn't proficient with the rifle but he felt safer with it across his saddle. He searched his surroundings constantly, listening, watching the dun's ears. He had learned they were the first to pick up trouble.

In an hour Wash recognized landmarks on his own spread. The tracks were faint. In places it seemed as if something had been dragged over them. Are they trying to cover the tracks? he wondered. See-sawing back and forth he finally picked them up again, now leading straight toward two buttes that touched each other.

He pulled the rifle up, letting his knees guide the dun.

Suddenly he felt foolish. What could one man do if he encountered those gun-slinging hands . . . probably joined by several others by now? Too late to think about that. The dun's ears flicked forward and he raised that muzzle for a smell. Wash pulled him slowly around a thick hedge of stinkweed. Here, they could hear the far-away mooing of contented cattle.

They were in front of a small opening between the two buttes. Wash couldn't believe it but the faint sound of the lowing cattle was coming through that crack. The beeves must have gone through that narrow five-foot opening.

His hands were wet as he nudged the stallion into the cut. If the rustlers had a guard he'd be shot as he entered.

Evidently they had no guard. He went safely through the break which opened out onto a low flat-bottomed valley. Wash whistled softly. It was fantastic. Even now in the late dry summer the meadow had grass. Cattle grazed and moved about at ease. There was a stand of aspen were water evidently flowed from the hills to the north.

"I'll be damned," Wash whispered. "So this is the holding pen of Jack Whelper. On my own spread. . . ."

He glanced quickly around the valley, searching for the crew. Behind a group of steers near the trees he spotted a cook wagon with five or six men around it, some sitting, talking, others working on tack or playing with a rope. To one side a branding fire glowed.

His rifle might get a single man but he'd be pinned against this flat-backed boulder like a coon caught in lantern light. He needed an idea.

Suddenly he recalled a character in one of the stories

his father had often told him when they lived at the academy. A small boy was confronted by bandits in the woods. The boy had nothing with which to defend himself. He was fishing with only a can of worms. But he was noted for hollaring louder than any kid in town. And he had an idea. The lad picked up a stick and beating the tin can and shouting at the top of his lungs, he plowed through the bandits' camp, scattering them right and left.

Wash grinned, remembering how he and his father had laughed and how Wash begged for him to tell it, "Again, again".

"Why not give it a try," Wash whispered to the dun. "You can run, I can make noise. Let's go."

"Waaahoooing" at the top of his lungs and sending a volley of rifle shots before them, Wash kneed the stallion into a full gallop down the hill into the valley. He swerved around a bunch of startled steers, cut back into a line toward the wagon, firing into the air and shouting. As he neared the camp he shoved the rifle into the boot and drew his pistol. The frightened cowboys were caught flat-footed. One dived for cover, another dropped the skillet he was holding and stood agast. Two lunged for their guns and began firing.

Twenty-five yards before the cookfire Wash aimed the .45 and as he and the hell-bent-for-leather mustang raced through the camp he downed the man firing the rifle. Curses rang into the hot afternoon air. Cattle began mooing, at least a dozen took to their heels and knocked over the cook wagon on their way to the far side of the valley.

Wash continued to yell, firing now on his left. He shot the skillet out of the hands of the cook who for some reason had picked it up again. Then leaning low over the saddle Wash missed getting hit himself by inches while his back was to the camp.

Once through the debris of the trampled campsite, Wash turned the dun in a spinning arc, dug in his heels and raced back through the cursing, yelling cowhands. This time he aimed at the one in the yellow shirt who stepped in front with a blazing Winchester. A bullet wizzed by the dun's left ear and Wash shot the legs out from under the yellow shirt.

Wash's loud "Hyah! Hyah!" encouraged the last cowboy to fall and roll for safety as Wash raced by. He lowered the pistol now and booting the mustang with a staccato of hits, he fled for the opening between the buttes.

They skidded through the narrow defile with Wash's knees scraping rock. They came out on the south side intact and heaving. Wash let the dun slow down, but he couldn't stop. He needed to get well away, to lose any trackers. Around the low hills on their right he met the rocky slough he recognized. He and Smoke had stood there as she pointed out Diamond Peak.

Now for the hidden safety of that cedar break he remembered near the Yellow Cat!

Chapter Twenty-six

He was under the cottonwoods near the cabin. Evidently Whelper had not yet traced Briley to the mountain. But it whouldn't be long before this place was no longer safe.

Wash had a headache. He felt sick. The surge of energy—and even excitement—that rushed through him during that impossible attack was gone. Left in its place was a sinking feeling. He'd succumbed to the rage that seemed to reside under the skin of these western men, inflaming their need to wreak revenge with force.

He'd killed a man. Or maybe two, and wounded others. He hadn't thought about it as it happened. Now it washed over him in waves of sickness. Damn that Whelper for making him an outlaw as violent as himself.

Elizabeth would shudder along with him if she knew what had happened. Her idea of taking up a gun was a romantic notion, not one that counted the dangers and death it carried with it.

Well, it was done. He was committed. He would see it through.

Asa was braying. When Briley rode in, the burro greeted the line-back dun with a nip on the shoulder and the two began to graze side by side.

"You have any luck?" Briley asked, easing himself onto the sitting stump.

"Some," Wash said. He told Briley about the theft of Crowder's cattle and the chase to the holding pen. When Wash told Briley the stash of stolen cattle was on his own spread, back of the far north buttes, Briley whistled. "That there is why he wants you gone ain't it?"

"Seems so. He has a neat set-up. He rustles the beeves quickly and quietly off his neighbor's land, not bothering to brand 'em, then sweeps them into that hidy hole to await his pleasure. Being able to stash away the stolen beef until the new brands heal and he gets ready to drive them across his own land to the rails has kept Whelper from the law. But why he should be so afraid of me I don't know. Like everyone else, I'd never have found that hidden meadow."

Briley chuckled. "You're a eastern dude all right. But Buchanan, you got a way about you that is might near fearsome jist because it's so dee-termined. Whelper's always been able to shy people away with threats til you come."

Wash thought of his grandfather. He hadn't shied away. He got himself killed for it too. He looked up at Briley. "I shot one of his ruffians, Briley. Wounded others. Whelper will be after me now with fire in his gut."

Briley cut a plug. "Thought you seemed hung-over.

And knowin' you don't drink, I wondered. Don't worry, boy, you'll get used to it."

"Rather not." Wash's head dropped and he raked stiff fingers through his hair.

After a moment Briley said, "I got word to your gal and she's gonna get that Elizabeth lady to send the telegram to the Marshall in Cheyenne."

"Good." Wash sat up. "The Drennans will have more influence than I had. My telegram must have been stopped."

"I give him three days to git here or we'd take care of the business ourselves. But that seems right down foolish now I think about it.

"And Buchanan, seems there's a new gun workin' with Whelper now."

Wash nodded. "I know. I've seen him. I saw him shoot that young fellow, one of Delight's cowboys. The gun's name is Elliott 'Bull' Nettles though I can't see why they'd tag him 'Bull'. He's smaller than me."

Briley spit then asked, "You never got stung by a bull nettle?"

"I've seen 'em but no, never got stung by one."

"Welts as big as your hand raise up all over you and you git chills and sweats. It's a right terrible thing to tackle a bull nettle, son."

"Then that fits. That man's got no blood in his bones, Briley. He's all pure reaction. He'd as soon reach out and sting you as not, doesn't matter to him. He'll be the one to deal with if it comes to a showdown."

"Then you better practice," Briley advised. "Whilst I put on the grub. Figure we can rest up for a day then hit the trail for Whelper's place so's we'll be there by the time the Marshall arrives."

As he passed, Briley glanced at the stallion. "That dun any better mount?"

Wash studied the dun, his stubby, crooked legs, his ugly, scarred neck, and that coarse, upstanding mane. "Yea. He'll do," he said.

Asa was left behind. She protested mightily until a bucket of grain was placed before her. She settled her nose in it with single-minded determination.

On the first day's ride through the buttes and into the mountainous range of the Yellow Cat River, they pushed hard. They were a silent, thoughtful pair, each goaded by his personal reasons for the vendetta. By late afternoon they were sweaty and tired, a grim spectacle.

Wash found himself impatiently reprimanding the dun for a stumble or for trying to grab at tufts of switchgrass as they passed. His back ached from being held tightly upright, on guard, waiting for trouble.

As they entered a rocky valley nestled in the lemon-colored hills, the dun began to shy and prance, his ears straight and still.

The peel of an eagle rang overhead. Loose shale tumbled downslope from their right. "Bad country," Briley called back. "Mountain cats in these hills. Rein thet dun in tight!"

"I'm liable to do the opposite," Wash muttered. "Best let this cantankerous animal have his freedom if a cat comes."

The stallion whickered, stomping from side to side. He kept glancing at the gully that cut in front and to the left and probably headed for the upper regions of that mountain.

"Where does it go, boy? You been here before or just

scared of what you smell?" Wash asked the horse who was now walling white-rimmed eyes and tossing his head, flinging foam from his nostrils, trying to git rid of the hated smell.

He's about to bolt, Wash decided.

He slid off, unbuckled the saddle and pack and let them drop. He pulled the bridle over the dun's twisting head and stepped back.

For a moment the dun pawed the hard rock floor and blew out through his nose. Then a piercing human scream rent the air and the mustang began to trot steadily up the alley, into the higher rocks.

Briley had turned, was looking back. "Whut in tarnation!" he exclaimed.

"Gone after that cat I reckon," Wash said with a shake of his head. "You wait here and I'll follow a piece. See if he's gone forever or if that cat finishes what he probably started years ago."

"Wouldn't try it," Briley warned.

But Wash had plucked the rifle out of the boot and was climbing, bent over, his gaze searching overhead. His hands were wet on the rifle butt, his heart a pulsing drum beat. Where are you? he wondered. Then he could hear the threatening whinny of his horse overlayed by the growling and screaming cry of the cat.

Wash lifted the rifle as he rounded another towering rock.

He stood still. He was at the opening of a walled-in room. His drum-beating heart stopped completely at the sight before him. Head erect, the dun pranced in a circle before a perpendicular wall of yellow sandstone. At the top of the wall Wash could see the prone body of a large puma, her eyes red with anger, her tail switching against the hot rocks.

Wash froze. He did not trust himself to aim the rifle and fire precisely into the head of that cat. And the dun could never escape once the animal had him around the neck. "By the holy goodness," Wash muttered as the cat raised her haunches and leaped from her perch onto the whistling mustang.

Wash stumbled backward and raised the rifle. But the two combatents had closed his chance of firing. The cat clung to the stallion, clawing new ridges down that ugly neck, struggling to find a grip with her inch-long fangs.

The dun whirled about, reared up, bucked with all the force of his ancient, remembered hurt.

Then he turned and drove his bared teeth into the leg of the lion and she let go, fell to the ground.

Before she could scamper up, the mustang laid a front hoof across her head. She was stunned but she staggered up. The dun had turned and now he began kicking, bouncing the puma's hundred pound body against the mountain wall.

The limp body fell back to the ground and the dun kicked it again, sending it careening across the rocks. He whinnied and snorted and pawed the slack body, not satisfied until it lay still, its fight drained, its once red eyes blind and staring.

Wash's trembling legs collapsed and he sat down.

The dun trotted around the carcass, snorting and blowing.

Finally the mustang passed by the body with a single hit with one hoof, then walked past Wash through the alley into the open.

As soon as he found his breath, Wash followed.

The dun stood beside Briley, slightly quivering but evidently ready to continue their journey.

"What happened?" Briley asked, wiping the sweat off his face. "Sounded like a war up there."

Wash went to pick up the saddle. He couldn't answer.

Chapter Twenty-seven

Elizabeth and J. T. Drennan sipped after-dinner wine at Delmonicos. Elizabeth was jittery, unable to enjoy their usual conversation. "Dad," she finally said, "I would like to talk to that girl at the livery. Maybe she'll know something new about Washington."

"It's getting late," J. T. announced, glancing at his watch. "Be quick about it and I'll pick you up in a few minutes."

Elizabeth took long strides toward the livery at the end of the street. These past two weeks had been nerve-wracking since they'd heard first that Wash was dead, and later that he was alive. And the last two days when her father had gone to Cheyenne to see Marshall Clifton O'Rear had put tiny lines under her eyes. She'd not slept a full night since.

Her father had insisted he go to the marshall in person rather than risk another telegram that would not reach its destination. He also wanted the marshall to know the facts of the situation from the point of view of an objective business man "of some standing" in the community.

During the last few days Elizabeth had shopped, helped Eliza with the cleaning and cooking, and now had nothing to do. She needed to talk to someone. Even Smoke Rising.

Of course the girl had fallen for Washington. She'd undoubtedly never been around anyone of his caliber and naturally she'd tumble. But it piqued Elizabeth to think of it.

Nevertheless, Smoke Rising was rather interesting and certainly a lovely girl with those dark, dark blue eyes. Maybe she would have later news of Washington.

The livery doors were open but no lamps had been lit and early evening shadows darkened the place. A horse whinnied as if frightened. A water bucket had overturned and the sandy floor was scuffed and trampled as if a fight had taken place.

The rank musty smell was thick and Elizabeth put her handkerchief over her nose and began to walk down the central aisle. She hesitated to call. An uneasy feeling made her skin crawl. Something had happened here.

She thought she heard scuffling noises from outside. Then men's voices and a short, startled cry.

Stepping to the back entrance she looked out into the alley. Three horses and a mule were ground-reined. Their riders off-mounted, were talking in short gutteral pronouncements. One was tying a heavy gunnysack onto the back of the mule. The other three were coming toward Smoke Rising who stumbled and half turned to stop them.

"Smoke. . . ." Elizabeth started to call and stopped

short as the men grabbed the girl, yanked another gunny sack over her head and tied it swiftly around and around her body. Then picking her up like a sack of mule feed, they threw her onto the back of one of the horses.

"Look!" The huge man Elizabeth had learned was called Slick Matthews nodded toward her.

Lewis Whelper glared, then broke into a grin. "Good," he said. Elizabeth had met Lewis. Her father had sold him wire. He stepped close to her, holding the reins of his horse while the others were stamping impatiently, turning about in the dust of the alley. "Tell Buchanan he can find out what he needs to know at the Whelper ranch.

"Let's go boys." He climbed into the saddle and led the way down the alley. "Easy pickings!" the stoop-shouldered hombre bragged over his shoulder. "Meet us at the ranch. . . ."

"Or the sticks, hee, hee," the last man laughed and swaying in the saddle as if he were drunk, nearly fell off his horse.

Elizabeth stood frozen, trying to take it all in. Jack Whelper's brother and his men were kidnapping Smoke Rising . . . and Ed Lowery as well! And they wanted Washington to know it.

At a creek some five miles into Whelper territory, Wash and Briley made camp. The horses were spent and they drank slow and long before being staked in a small patch of green-topped weeds.

Wash cleaned the still-bleeding gashes on the dun's muzzle and neck. They were not deep, just long and liable to get infected. Wash talked as he swabbed bacon fat and suger over them.

"Well," he addressed the dun eye to eye. "You sure

surprised me, oh great Sheerkohf, Lion of the Mountain. Yes sir, that was some fight. Never knew a bronc to *ask* for a fight. But that cat didn't stand a chance. No sir, not with Killer here after her. Hold still, now Killer, hold still."

Wash stood back wanting to make sure he'd covered every scratch. When he was satisfied he dropped his swabbing rag and pulling the dun's face to him, hugged the startled animal around the neck.

Briley heard the conversation and smiled. "Finally got around to givin' the critter a name? Killer, huh?"

"He deserves it." Wash had not yet told Briley about the fight. Maybe he never would.

They took no chances with a fire but ate dried beef and biscuits. Not having coffee was a sacrifice they'd willingly make to keep the Whelpers from finding their camp.

"Whelper'll be guardin' the road and then probley have them guns in a circle round the house. Too, we'll be ridin' under look-out points from now on, I reckon," Briley informed Wash as they spread their blankets.

Wash laid his rifle beside his blanket and his colt touching his hand. Neither took off their boots and the horses were still saddled. They'd have to sleep standing up.

"I'm surprised we're not surrounded right now," Briley muttered as he balanced his Winchester against a rock and stretched out along side.

Wash glanced at the dun, he'd watch those ears and that head, hoping the mustang would warn them in time. "Whelper is not a straight-shooter, Briley. He'll have something fishy planned. We need to expect anything from now on."

"You seem purty sure we'll be ready," Briley said,

turning his back to the rock so he'd have a view of the open prairie. "You not afraid, boy?"

Wash chuckled. "I'm beginning to think fear is just the reverse side of getting the job done. And flippin' the coin can sometimes be accomplished in a day."

"Thet's a high-falutin' way o' sayin' you finally appreciate that line-back dun?" Wash was silent for a moment then he said, "Yea, I guess so."

Chapter Twenty-eight

The last few miles were through a piece of land fed by a creek. Then they rode on a gradual rise until low hills came in view.

"Three more o' these rises and we'll be at Whelper's back door." Briley spoke in a quiet voice. The morning ride had been undisturbed by riders guarding the land. No spark of rifle or sight of tracks indicated anyone watching.

This only sharpened the men's senses, made both of them look a little harder and sit a little higher. Both Briley and Wash had a rifle balanced over the pommel of their saddles.

By the time they reached the third rise they had a good view of the Whelper house. Wash's finger played lightly on the trigger of the Winchester, but the long front porch was clear. The cattle pens stood empty. No one was riding the yards.

"Spooky," whispered Briley. "I've a notion to fill that

house full o' shot and drive 'em out." His anger rose as he thought how close he was to getting revenge for a life of frustration and hurt. But he still hankered for his show-down.

"That may be what they want, Briley," Wash drop-reined the dun. "I'll ease around the other side and we'll come up together on the porch . . . if we get that far without being ambushed."

Circling the yard and cutting through an open barn where he expected to meet fire at every corner, Wash eased up to the far side of the house. He could hear nothing inside. No lights burned. No smoke from the cook-stove filled the air.

Turning, Wash glimpsed Briley scooting across an open area. Still no shots.

At a sign from Wash they began walking toward the front door, pistols drawn. A knot was kicking around inside Wash but his hand was steady, his mind clear.

"Like to talk, Whelper!" he yelled. Their own scuffling boots was the only answer. Wash tried the door. It opened easily and he pushed it in.

Entering the dark room, he saw a man seated at the table. His head was bent over as if in prayer. But he was tied, starting at the shoulders, in the straight-backed chair.

"Lowery!" Wash uttered. Quickly glancing into the other rooms, he holstered his gun and he and Briley cut the hostler loose.

A low, sick groan showed him still alive. He'd been beaten and knifed, blood oozed steadily from a gunshot wound in his stomach.

"Why you, Lowery?" Wash asked, raising the man's head for the water Briley held.

"So . . . so you'd believe. . . ." His words were ragged and faint. Beads of sweat dotted his forehead and his hands felt clammy to Wash. Not a good sign.

"Believe what?" Wash asked through gritted teeth.

"Business. They mean business." He coughed and blood drooled from his mouth. "Wanted me to tell you . . . tell you they got the girl. They took Smoke Rising." Ed Lowery's hurting eyes filled with tears and he sobbed. "Sorry I couldn't help her. I couldn't help her."

Wash glanced at Briley then said, "It's all right, Lowery. Where is she? Where have they taken her? We'll get her."

"No!" The wounded man struggled to sit. "That's why they left me—to tell you—to tell you to sign that there paper and then leave Granite Canyon." Lowery stared down at a paper weighted down with a frying pan near the edge of the table.

Wash picked up the official-looking document of sale, assigning his land to one Jack R. Whelper. The space for his signature was underlined.

"They expect me to sign this in exchange for Smoke's life?"

Lowery nodded. "Yes . . . yes. Or they'll do her like they done me." Lowery sobbed again.

Then he rallied to say, "Promise you'll sign and leave, Buchanan. Promis. . . ." Ed Lowery's head dropped, he slumped onto the table and spoke no more.

Wash's face was white, his mouth a tight line as he and Briley set about making a fire in the iron stove in the kitchen, putting on coffee.

Wash had searched the yard and grounds and found no tracks leading away. The kidnappers made sure to cover those. He was worried in a different way now. How best to save Smoke? If he did as Whelper wanted and signed that deed, and left, Whelper would not keep any promise to free the girl unharmed. Wash was certain of that.

His original plan to find the murderers and bring them in had shifted. Now he would neither wait for, nor ask for, a surrender. He would shoot first, ask questions later. But smoke Rising would have to be safe.

Over coffee, he and Briley decided not to take Lowery's body in to the sheriff. Nor call him out here. A useless ploy. "I'll stay here and take care o' Lowery. You go into town and check with thet girl Elizabeth," Briley said. "See if she sent for the marshall and mayhap you can see if those bushwackers might have Smoke Risin' some place near town." Wash knew Briley did not believe this was a possibility, but he too agreed with the plan.

Whatever they did, Whelper was waiting for them to make the next move.

If Whelper had any of his boys posted in town, there was no sign of it. It was after the noon hour and shades were drawn against the heat. Siestas were in progress, activity at a standstill.

Killer took in the strange smells of town like an old timer, ears up and nostrils quivering, but steady and sure-footed.

The double doors of the livery were shut with a note tacked to them. It said, GONE FOR VACATION.

At the back, Wash managed to open the simple latch and get inside. There were scores of footprints and horse prints and near one of the stalls there was evidence of a scuffle, but Wash found nothing that might indicate where they were holding Smoke Rising.

An urgency quickened his heartbeat. He hurried to latch the door. He wanted to get on and finish this business.

He tied the dun and went up the white steps of the Drennan house. A small black girl in a maid's apron answered his knock. She'd fetch Miss Drennan if he'd please wait in the parlor.

Funny, he thought, he felt ill at ease in this room with its velvet setee and fringed gold lamps and rug imported from Europe. Then he looked down at his pants covered with sugar-grease and the stick-tite seeds of prairie weeds. He studied his once elegant leather boots now scuffed and showing a tear on one side. Not so funny after all, he concluded. He'd have to get back in city duds soon or he'd lose his feel for fine things.

"Oh Washington," Elizabeth cried. She hurried in, looking with uncertain, red-rimmed eyes at him as she stepped into his embrace. "They have Smoke Rising." She pulled away as soon as she had blurted out her message.

"I know," he said, a frown creasing his forehead. "But how did you find out?"

"I . . . I saw it, Washington." She was distraught, on the verge of tears as she touched the back of the chair for him to sit. "I didn't know what to do. I knew the sheriff wouldn't help and I was afraid whatever I did would hurt you . . . so I . . . oh."

"You did right by keeping quiet," he assured her. "Just tell me what you saw."

"I went to tell Smoke Rising that we sent the message to Marshall O'Rear—in fact daddy took it himself and the Marshall is coming, Washington, he's coming. But before I could speak to Smoke Rising I saw these men in the alley hefting a sack onto a mule and then they grabbed her too." When Elizabeth gasped and shuddered, Wash poured a drink from the table near the window and made her drink it.

She hiccupped and finally said, "They had her tied in one of those horrible gunny sacks . . . just like Ed Lowery. It *was* Ed Lowery wasn't it, Washington?"

Wash nodded and she continued, "Then Lewis Whelper recognized me. And he didn't seem upset at all, but told me to inform you that you could meet them at their ranch."

Wash sighed. That much was not new. "Briley and I found Lowery at the Whelper house this morning, Elizabeth. He's dead."

She leaned back in her chair and closed her eyes. After a minute she sat up and asked, "Who is Briley?'

"A man who hates the Whelpers as much as I do. He's helping me. Now, Elizabeth, think. Is there anything else you know that might help me find Smoke Rising. Has anyone in town said anything? One of your father's friends or. . . ."

She shook her head adamantly.

Wash added, "Lowery was the only one at the Whelper house. And he had no idea where they've taken her." He hesitated, then decided Elizabeth needed to know everything. "They left a deed for me to sign, giving Whelper my spread. If I sign it and leave town, they say they won't harm her."

Elizabeth dobbed her eyes with a handkerchief, shaking her head in short nervous twitches of disbelief. Wash studied her worried face. She was really concerned for

Smoke and she was not breaking down. He felt suddenly ashamed. He'd not thought of her in days. She would be a good wife to have at a man's side, a partner who would stand through thick or thin.

"You have no idea where they were heading?"

She squinted, remembering something. "Other than that last man who was evidently drunk. He said something about heading for 'The Sticks'."

" 'The Sticks'?"

"I have no idea where that is, Washington."

He thought for a moment then said, "Potter will know. He's Simmons' man and he took me over my place when I first got here. Let's go find him. You need to know where the place is too so that . . . and if . . . the marshall gets here you can tell him where we are."

He picked up his hat and as he turned, Elizabeth caught him by the arm and stared up at him. "Washington," she said, "You look so . . . so different. I hardly knew you when I came in and saw you today." She gazed into his hard, flint-cold eyes, studied his sunburned, ruddy hands, stared at the gun and holster tied to his leg. "You did get a gun after all."

Wash's lips tightened. His shoulders slumped and he looked suddenly older. "Took your advice, Elizabeth. Seems I had to."

They went to find Potter.

Chapter Twenty-nine

Evening shadows elongated in front of horse and rider as they loped into the yard of the Whelper ranch.

The enticing aroma of woodsmoke floated from the chimney of the cookstove and Wash felt the pangs of hunger. He'd not eaten since early dawn and despite his anxious worry he knew he should eat and rest.

Briley had a pot of beans and beef simmering, and corn pones frying in a skillet. "May as well make ourselves to home, far as I see," he drawled when Wash stepped inside. "Besides, haven't set to a good supper in a while and I always track better on a full stomach."

"May not need to track, Briley, if you can get us near some place people call McKitchen pass."

Briley forked a crisp-fried corn pone onto a plate and ladled up beans and beef. "Know it. It's northwest from Fort Laramie. Why?"

"Elizabeth saw Whelper's men take Lowery and

Smoke Rising, and one of them mentioned 'The Sticks.' Ever hear of that?"

Briley wiped his hands on a huge white rag he'd tied around his waist. "Can't say I have. That past the McKitchens?"

"According to Frank Potter it is. He says The Sticks is a ten acre draw with a stand of scrubby, half-dead pines that look like match sticks. It's an isolated place, perfect for holding a girl kidnapped.

"J. T. Drennan went to the marshall in Cheyenne so maybe he'll show up. Whether he does or doesn't we'll go on in. That okay with you?"

"Oh yea. Guns is oiled and loaded."

"You think we're being watched?" Wash asked as he wiped up the last bit of gravy with his cornbread.

"Yep. Think I saw one move on the hill when I put Lowery down yesterday. But they're jus waitin' fer us to decide whut to do with this here deed. You gonna sign it?"

Wash took his plate to a table and dunked it in a pan of water. "No. Whelper would not keep any bargain like that, as you well know. I'll take it with me though and when we leave in the morning we'll head toward town, packs and all as if we're going to do what he wants. We'll turn back when we've dusted our tail."

Briley nodded and the two men blew out the lantern and crawled into the bunks.

Midmorning, they were on a swing north of the edge of Whelper's spread, just south of the North Platte. "Those are the McKitchens," Briley said, pointing to a bridge of low hills.

Silently they rode between the breaks in the hills,

winding their way nearer those needle-pointed trees called The Sticks.

They passed into a cedar grove atwitter with thrushes and sparrows feeding on bugs and seed. Streaks of yellow sun lit up the needled floor and the stringent odor of the cedars and pines filled the soft morning air. The day would be clear and hot. A day for cattle roping, or for catching a twelve-mare manada. Or a day for being with a woman who would ride beside you.

"Not a day for killing," flashed through Wash's mind.

Nearing the last of the rolling hilltops, Briley motioned "up" and Wash slid off the dun who was still calm, his ears flopping easily. No one close yet, it seemed. But Wash was silent as he climbed the hill Briley had indicated. He lay on his stomach at the edge, with a good view of the tall, thin trees in the draw.

He raised the glasses Elizabeth had given him and studied the hollow below. He could see the trunks and broken limbs and half-green needles of the pines that grew so thick they touched in places. There was no movement, no horses, no smoke.

But there must be water somewhere inside that wilderness or Whelper wouldn't stay more than a day . . . he loves his comfort too much. So where? Wash wondered.

He swung the glass to his far right. He noticed a deep gully cutting into the edge of the pines. He ajusted the lens and could now see the green sides of the gully, a sign of grass or weeds, a sign of water, probably a ground-fed creek. The most likely spot for a camp, Wash concluded.

Heat waves suddenly distorted his view and he moved the field glasses to higher terrain between his hill and the last one. A movement caught his attention and he focused tighter. A man sat on a bluff some two hundred yards to the left, at the beginning of the trees.

Another was perched near the edge of the ravine they would pass to reach The Sticks.

Wash crawled back to Briley. "Looks like only two guards. You take the one on the hill. I'll get the one near the entrance. Then we'll go together through that far gully. It should be a creekbed leading into the pines. Ready?"

Together they hunkered around the hill, loaded with bullets, rifles and each carrying a newly honed knife.

It must be noon, Wash decided as he edged his way through the rocks and short hedge-like bushes along the open pass. No sign of good Marshall Clifton O'Rear. Well, they'd make do.

Sweat dripped off his face and he wondered if Smoke was thirsty. He prayed she was all right. Not like Ed Lowery.

At the thought of Lowery and what Whelper had done to that innocent man, Wash clenched his hand around the knife and hunkered close to the hillside, readying himself for a hand-to-hand fight.

He climbed the last few feet between himself and the guard. The man was sitting, watching, but his rifle lay to one side. Wash did not need the knife. He dropped to his knees and when the man pulled a smoke from his pocket, Wash leaped up and laid the butt of his rifle across the back of the man's head.

It was one of the regular hands he'd seen at the ranch . . . not Stoop or Slick, or Nettles. Wash was glad he'd not had to kill this one. He broke out leather strips and bound the man's feet, his hands in back, then dragged him under a tree.

Wash was breathing hard. He slid down the hill and running, cut to the gully. Briley was there, wiping his knife. "Had to," he answered Wash's raised eyebrows.

Wash had been right, a thin trickle of ground water seeped into the ravine near the stand of pines. Wash looked up the path the shallow cut formed and held up his hand. Fifty yards into the pines it forked. Wash pointed to the right and nodded at Briley.

Wash took the left fork, hunched over now, glancing carefully on every side. He carried the rifle in his left hand, his right hovering near the .45.

He was about to enter the trees on his left when from out of a curve in the shallow ravine three horses appeared. The riders pulled to a halt and one yelled, "It's Buchanan!"

The men, crazed with rage, yelled and fired and drove their mounts toward Wash, slipping on the gully floor.

A hot fiery sting on his right side whirled Wash on his toes and sent him plunging up the shallow bank. Two riders fired at once and sent bark flying off the tree beside him.

Dropping his rifle, Wash chose the first man riding a paint—it was stoop Ragan. With a fist of hate balling up in his gut, Wash drew and fired into the culprit's throat. Stoop flung his rifle to the wind and fell to the ground.

The remaining two horses bunched together, their riders firing at once. Slugs peppered the forest floor behind Wash who had crossed the gully in front of the frightened pinto. He turned to put a bullet into the nearest man. Then without moving he thumbed back the hammer, knocking the last bushwacker out of the saddle with a slug boring a black hole in his heart.

The horses fled with the help of a slap on their rumps and Wash tore through the woods separating him from Briley.

Briley was in a niche of soft sand formed by the deepening channel. "Whut happened?" he muttered.

"Three riders." Wash was panting. His heart was racing and he needed a drink. "You find anything?"

Briley hunched his head forward to see the gully up ahead and said in Wash's ear, "There's a cabin. No one outside. I got a looksee in a back window. She's there. Tied and layin' on the floor."

Wash took a deep breath. "Who's with her?"

"Both Whelpers in one corner arguin'. Thet bald mountain o'va man, and that gun you say is Bull Nettles. He wus cleanin' a pistol."

"What did they do when they heard the shots?"

"Baldy and Lewis took off but I didn't see Jack or Nettles leavin'."

Wash was nervous. His skin itched, waiting for Lewis or Brute to appear. He checked his .45 and sighed with relief. He'd automatically reloaded as Briley had demanded when teaching him. He didn't remember doing it.

"You watch for Lewis and Brute in case they're still outside. I'll try to get inside and take Jack and Bull. Let's go."

They slipped quickly into the thick trees beside the cabin. A string line held four horses at the back. Evidently Lewis and Slick Matthews, the brute, were still afoot. Wash silently cut the ties of the horses and shoved them off with his bare hand. They moved slowly toward the back woods and dropping their heads began to crop the short grass.

Briley, watching for Lewis and Brute, saw no movement in the trees anywhere around the house, and nodded all clear.

Near the window, Wash waved Briley beside him. They dared not glance inside this time . . . hearing the gunfire, Whelper was alert now and would be checking the window. He'd not hesitate to shoot and a .44 could easily pierce the thin walls of the cabin.

But they could hear mutterings, Whelper cursing and telling Bull to "Get yourself into that corner and be ready when they come." Smoke groaned, mumbled as if gagged, and Whelper snarled, "Keep quiet and stand up here in front of me." A slap. Then, "Be still, I said."

He must be using Smoke as a shield. Hot anger coursed through Wash and he bowed his head to steady himself. The afternoon sun had passed its zenith. Fence-like patterns of the trees on the cabin reminded Wash of a jail. Would he get her out alive?

Briley, edging toward the door, brought Wash to his senses and he shook his head at Briley. They dared not rush in.

Then Wash's eyes fell on the remains of a broken-down wagon, it's wheels off, the tongue lying near the frontside of the cabin. The tongue and axle formed a cross.

Wash holstered his .45 and motioning for Briley to help, they each took hold of the long axle and turned the front piece toward the door.

Briley understood without a word what Wash wanted.

Looking into his eyes, Wash signaled to heave. On the third swing they slammed the front tongue into the flimsy door and it split apart. Shots zinged through the opening but Wash and Briley had jumped aside.

Then Whelper was shouting, "Shoot them, you buzzard!" And Bull Nettles stomped out the broken door firing both six-guns in a barrage of bullets that made the air zizzle.

Briley was nearest, facing Bull, and he immediately dropped to the ground and rolled. "Don't let me be shot," flew through Wash's mind as he too scooted out of range of the mad-man's fire.

Wash got off a shot as he scooted backward. It sailed past the grinning little man who marched further into the yard, turned and glared at Wash as if to say, "Here I am."

Suddenly shots came from the woods. Lewis and Brute had stopped at the clearing and were down on their knees firing toward the house.

Whelper's crazed yell from inside commanded the shooting to stop, but his brother and cohort fired at will, peppering the front of the cabin with bullets.

Lying flat on the ground, Briley kept raising the dragoon, sending slugs overhead toward the woods. Evidently he wasn't dead . . . not yet.

Wash scooted quickly behind the fallen wagon, fired several shots toward Brute and Lewis then waited. He had only one more bullet without reloading and Bull Nettles was circling the wagon.

Horses whinnied from the gully side, men yelled, and shots rang out as a huge white gelding and a smaller black came charging into the open.

Wash hesitated a second, then Bull Nettles was ten feet in front of him, raising one of those steaming Peacemakers. But without thinking, Wash had already raised his Colt, thumbed back the hammer and blasted the grin off his face.

Wiping his fingers through his hair, Wash turned to see two men helping Briley stand. One wore a badge. He said something to Briley then let him go and stomped into the cabin, his gun drawn.

Breathing so shakily he could not move, Wash waited for the Marshall to call all-safe. Instead he appeared back in the doorway calling, "Man away. He's on a big steel-grey, headed north."

Chapter Thirty

The confusion in the small musty room was a muffled cacophony of noise as Wash searched the faces. The marshall, still wearing his huge stetson and a hastily wrapped handkerchief around his wrist where a bullet had nicked him, was handcuffing Lewis Whelper. Jack's smaller brother was whining in a drone that made Wash want to slap his face.

In another corner the deputy was talking to Elizabeth and J. T. who had ridden recklessly up at the last minute.

Finally Wash pushed his way to Smoke, huddled in a blanket on the floor, rocking back and forth. Her shirt was torn off one shoulder and her face and neck were scratched and covered with bruises. Wash lifted her into a chair and pulled the blanket over her shoulder. "You're all right now" he repeated over and over.

"Let me take her, Wash. We've a buggy coming along soon and we'll drive her in to town." Elizabeth began to wipe Smoke Rising's face with a wet cloth.

Wash mumbled, "Okay, thanks," and turned to the marshall. "I'm going after Whelper, Marshall O'Rear. It's just a matter of wearing him down and one can do it as well as three. Briley can tell you about everything here."

The marshall looked around the room, then outside at the body of Slick. Recalling something about other bodies in the fork of the ravine and on the hill and near the rocks, he said, "Wish you'd wait but seein' you're not I'll track you soon's I can."

Wash stopped outside and spoke to Briley, "I'm after him and I want you to see that Smoke is taken care of. The Drennans will do it but . . ."

"Yea. Will do. You sure you don't want company? He's ridin' Brute's big steel. He can outrun any horse we got . . . including the dun, yuh know."

"But that mustang can outlast any horse alive, including the steel. I'll bring Whelper back for you if I can, Briley."

"Just *you* come back," Briley said. The two friends looked at each other for an instant, then Wash ran to get the line-back.

The trail was easy to follow. Within two hours Wash had the big grey gelding Whelper was riding in sight. Whelper had already made the mistake of scaling the five-hundred foot side of a rocky butte trying to hide his tracks. Wash knew he'd come out due east onto the plain again, so he kept to low ground and was on the murderer's heels when he descended.

The gelding was a large, raw-boned, long-legged horse and like Briley said, could easily outrun Killer. But Whelper was not thinking straight, he was trying to fool his tracker, and in doing so only made it easy to keep up.

Wash settled back in the saddle for a long ride. His side was hurting and when he put his hand inside his shirt it came away bloody. Darn! He'd been shot sometime during that bewildering fight. "I don't need that," Wash mumbled and felt the first scalding pain that would plague him for the next few hours.

He stuffed his handkerchief against the bloody wound, wishing he had some of Jake's black gooey tar and sulphur. The side throbbed and he was getting hot. But he concentrated on the trail and swore the gunshot would not keep him from going after Jack Whelper.

Whelper rode frantically now, without using his head. He skirted low, hilly, short-cuts and then slogged through cactus-shrouded plateaus full of prairie dog holes. Wash looked ahead, took easy routes and rode at a steady ground-eating cantor.

A bright full moon was up before the sun set. By nightfall Wash could still see well enough to maintain a fair distance from the gelding. A distance that gave him a glimpse of Whelper's figure which was either hunched over on the run or fidgeting in the saddle, turning back to locate his pursuer.

At a creek bed, the grey's feet had slipped on razor-sharp gravel and the horse had fallen. Wash took a breather when he saw it. That horse would be wobbly, maybe even hurt substantially. They'd both travel slower now.

Dismounted, Wash poured water from his canteen onto the handkerchief and swinging it in the air to cool it off, placed it gingerly against his side again. His eyes closed with the sting but he needed to prevent serious bleeding and he hoped the rag would do it.

When he climbed back into the saddle he felt dizzy, nearly fell. *Let me make it*, he silently pleaded. *I've gotta make it.*

The circling, erratic movements of Jack Whelper proved to Wash he was traveling on sheer panic. The man had no plans, no ultimate destination. As it was, they were headed for Fort Laramie.

Wash intended that Jack Whelper would not make it that far.

Wash drowsed. The mustang was smelling out their prey like a dog, and Wash let him have his way. Killer was in his element. He was well rested, had eaten grain, and was into that tireless, ceaseless gallop he could keep up for days. And it was a cool night with light enough for any wild creature.

Wash was bone tired. Deep exhaustion was settling in beside the dull pain that reached all the way to his back. Was the bullet still inside?

In his dazed half-sleep, the image of Smoke Rising with her torn shirt came to him, rousing in him the deepest anger he had ever felt. Smoke was innocent . . . as was Ed Lowery. As was his grandfather. But something made this anger different. Was it love? Did he love the girl?

Jogged into a state of near unconsciousness, Wash jerked to a start when he felt Killer slowing to a walk. The sun was up and the frightened whinny of a horse floated through the early morning air like some mournful premonition.

Wash gathered the reins in a hand that shook and slowly guided the dun toward a sink fifty feet ahead.

Water from underground seeps under a spot of deep black loam, plus the rains of the last few days, had made a thick, miry wallow.

Whelper and the gelding were down, the gelding sunk to his belly in the black mud. The panic-driven animal lunged upward, struggling to free himself. Whelper was knee-deep in the mire, pulling on the reins, shouting curses as he hit the stricken animal repeatedly with a stick. One of Whelper's knees was wrapped with a tight bandage on the outside of his pants. He favored the leg as he hobbled through the muck, hitting and cursing. His energies concentrated so malevolently on the poor creature, he failed to see Wash closing in.

Wash halted and stared. That horse was sinking, he'd never get free. Blood dripped from his nostrils and his eyes told Wash he was doomed.

Whelper suddenly raised his angry face and seeing Wash, he dropped the reins. Fumbling like a drunk man, he drew his pistol and fired.

Killer flinched as the bullet whizzed past. Wash's eyes squinted and he slid off the dun with a jolt that shocked him all the way to his teeth. A hot poker seared his side. He was bleeding into his pants.

He took a breath and walked up to the edge of the sinkhole. "Give it up Whelper and I'll take you in. Otherwise I'll put a bullet between your eyes."

"You and who else? Why didn't you leave? Why did you come out here in the first place? I want you dead!" Whelper was limping forward in the mud, waving that .45 over his head like a man possessed. Spit drooled from his mouth and his eyes drilled fire into Wash Buchanan.

"Stop," Wash said quietly.

"Die!" Whelper snarled, and grabbing his gun with both shaking hands, centered it on Wash's chest. He shouldn't have.

Wash was dizzy and burning with fever and his side felt like a house on fire. But he had been taught well. He didn't need to think or even see. His enemy was a dark shape and Wash's hand was invisible as it swung up and forward, pulling the .45 out and hammering it back in one sweet, beautiful move.

Whelper was knocked backward into the dank slush, and sank like the dead weight he was.

Chapter Thirty-one

Wash was wrong about the horse and he was glad. He left Whelper to his deserved, miry grave, but as the gallant grey called and struggled to free himself from the sink, Wash threw a rope around the saddle horn and clicking the dun backwards, was able to pull the steel from the sucking mire.

They spent the rest of the morning resting under a juniper tree. Wash drained his canteen then slept fitfully for half an hour. He woke, propped himself against the tree, not bothering to check the rag on his side. The bleeding had stopped, his pants were covered with dry, dusky red streaks of it.

As he gathered his wits to move out, Wash studied the tall, long-limbed horse Whelper had ridden. He reminded Wash of Hoshaba and why he had come to Wyoming. At the comparison Wash shook his head. Hoshaba had been killed by Jack Whelper. And this gelding, another great riding-horse, had taken his place to finish their confrontation. And yet—now Wash looked over at that stubby, knock-kneed mustang—and yet whelper was bested after all by the simple "usin' horse" of his own country. A native mustang of this wild, wonderful country.

It was late evening when Wash reached the outskirts of Granite Canyon. He swayed in the saddle, seeing two of everything: two lights moving through the darkness, two men on horseback, two faces looking down at him as he slid off Killer onto the ground.

When he came to himself Elizabeth was on one side of the bed, Smoke and Briley on the other. Elizabeth looked strange. Her eyes shone with worry and excitement combined.

"Oh thank heaven you're all right," she cried and bending over kissed his hot cheek.

Then he felt a small cool hand grip his own. Smoke Rising's eyes flashed when he looked up. A timorous flicker lifted her lips in the sweetest smile he'd ever seen. She was suddenly not the same haunted-faced girl he had left at the cabin. She was alive with some inner possession. She sparkled and glowed and her other small white hand held to Briley's rough-worn one with a grip that would never let go.

Wash lay stunned, confused.

Elizabeth came back into the room with her father and the marshall and the deputy trailing behind. The men stood silently at the foot of the bed as Elizabeth asked, "Did you kill him?"

Wash made his mind center on the events of the last two days. Whelper . . . he nodded yes.

"Good," she said and now that half-worried gleam in

her eye changed to pure excitement. Wash was bewildered.

She threw a quick glance at Smoke and Briley who still stood silent as a couple of thieves who'd just grabbed a sack of gold, then said, "Marshall O'Rear couldn't find your tracks, Washington, but as you remember they found you as you rode in and brought you here to my house."

Wash looked at Smoke, wanting never to take his eyes off her, hoping the others would go away, or at least be quiet. But Elizabeth had more to say. "Your money's waiting at the sheriff's office and Doc Grover says the bullet just dug a nice clean hole in a muscle. You'll be up and going in a few days."

Elizabeth smiled. O'Rear was still standing against the wall holding his big hat against his stomach. His deputy had his thumbs resting inside his belt. J. T. was jiggling his watch in one hand. No one seemed in a hurry to leave.

Briley glanced sheepishly down at Wash and then quickly back at Smoke whose hand he had begun to stroke and pat.

Wash was more than bewildered.

"Tell him, girl." J. T. finally said to his daughter and grinning furiously, Elizabeth cried, "We have discovered something so extraordinary and wonderful that it has . . . well, just skittled us over." She was now staring at Smoke and Briley who couldn't seem to take their eyes off each other.

"You tell him, Briley . . . that is, Jess Kendall." Everyone laughed and Wash began to sweat.

"Well," Briley stated, "When I got to a'tellin' the marshall about Whelper an' me. About me really bein'

Jess Kendall and my losin' Mary Rose and little Mary Argent . . . why Smoke here near 'bout fainted. She wails out thet she's a Kendall and she's Mary Argent Kendall left at the hogan o' one o' them Cheyenne Indans when she was just a tyke 'cause Mary Rose knowed the Indan to be a healer an' she and little Mary wus sick, see, an'. . . ."

Everyone laughed again and Smoke hugged his old hand to her face. Looking down at Wash she said, "He's my father, Wash. I found my father."

They stood beside Sister's stall. The dun and the grey were munching grain. Wash put his arm around the girl he had asked to be his wife and said, "Elizabeth isn't angry?"

"About you and me? No, Wash. She doesn't love you as I do. She's like another sister, she's one of God's creature's who can love everyone equally . . . until she finds someone she can love alone."

Wash stroked the tough black mane of the dun he'd named Killer and said, "We'll never know what could have come from Hoshaba and those mustang mares . . . that's what's so sad."

Smoke grinned and tossed her head to one side. "Oh, I don't know about that." She opened Sister's stall door and let the mare out into the alley. As she did, she touched the mustang's side and added, "Come spring, or thereabout, we'll see."